I0726269

She Fell in Love With a Boss

KEAIDY BENNETT

& REBEL FOXX

OTHER BOOKS BY KEAIDY BENNETT-SELMON

Charge it to the Game

Charge it to the Game 2: Tammy's Story

Charge it to the Game 3: Three Sides to Every Story

Charge it to the Game 4: Pride Comes B4 Destruction (Coming 2023)

Somewhere Between Love & Misunderstanding

The Chronicles of a Love Addict

When a Woman's Fed Up (Coming 2023)

Shut Up & Finish Your Book Already

JOIN OUR MAILING LIST!

Don't miss out when we release new books! Make sure to join our mailing list by texting **BOOKTRAP** to (407) 890-8882.

This is a work of fiction. Names, characters, businesses, places, events, and incidents are either the product of the author's imagination or used in a fictitious manner. Any resemblance to actual persons, living or dead, or actual events is purely coincidental.

Copyright © 2022 Keaidy Bennett & Rebel Foxx

All rights reserved. This book or any portion thereof may not be reproduced or used in any manner whatsoever without the express written permission of the publisher except for the use of brief quotations in a book review.

LexxiKhan Presents Publishing
www.LexxiKhanPresents.com

Ordering Information:
Quantity sales. Special discounts are available on quantity purchases by corporations, associations, and others. For details, contact the publisher at the web address above.

This book contains an excerpt from "When a Woman's Fed Up." It may be edited or deleted prior to actual publication.

ISBN-13: 978-1-958335-00-0

DEDICATION

To the women who are finally finding confidence in their own skin: we see you lil' mama.

Kinky

REBEL FOXX

PROLOGUE

The definition of a boss is simple. It's a person who exercises control or authority. Now, depending on where you grew up, it can change how you look at someone you consider to be a boss.

Growing up in an area we knew as "Crime Hills," in Orlando, Florida, a boss, to me, was a nigga that got *real* money - no matter the cost. I always figured that man had the resources to afford himself any kind of power or control he was seeking.

Although I was fortunate to be raised in a two-parent household where we never had to worry about the necessities of life, I had extremely expensive taste. That's why I hated watching other women in shit that I deserved to have too. I couldn't understand why some women's luxurious life was only a dream for women like me. I guess that's why when I discovered the power of my sexuality at fifteen, I used it to get all the things my parents couldn't afford for me to have.

After my first time dealing with a baller, I grew obsessed with the money and lifestyle of a street nigga. Did I know and truly understand the consequences? Hell no. Honestly, I didn't care about the choice someone else made. I had no aspiration to be a ride or die; I just cared about him financing all of my desires and wishes. What he had to do for the money I needed was for him and God to worry about one day. I just knew I had access to an endless supply of money, and everything I could ever want was in front of me. Why would I care about consequences?

Then, it happened. At eighteen, I decided to let my drug-dealing

1

boyfriend drive my car while we rode around the city. He was making sales, and along the way, I was blowing through his profits. Everything was all good until Orlando PD decided to put a stop to our run for the day.

When the police jumped behind us, I didn't even flinch. It wasn't my drugs; therefore, it wasn't my problem, right? Wrong! Ya'll aren't going to believe it, but this nigga had the audacity to let them search my shit and then deny the drugs they found. Now, at this point in my life, I had only ever been around street niggas. I was in no way "street smart," so when the officer came around to my side and told me to step out, all I wanted to do was cry and ask for my daddy. Although my father was not a rich nigga, he definitely was not a bitch nigga like the fool I had been riding around with.

Everything in me wanted to snitch on his scary ass, but I had read enough urban fiction novels to know that I might regret it later. Instead, I cried like a baby as the officer tried to force a confession out of me.

Unable to get what he was looking for, he decided to cuff us both to take us into the station. I really believe those cold, rigid, heavy cuffs are now the reason I hate wearing anything on my wrists.

Anyway, once we were downtown, I was allowed to make one phone call, and I was stuck. On one hand, I knew my father was always going to show up for his only child; however, his ass couldn't possibly have the money to get me out of the mess I had created for myself.

On the flip side, I knew if I called any of the other niggas I had been dealing with, I would have to explain why I was even in the car with the idiot I was arrested with. At that moment, despite how desperate I was, I decided to bet on my father. Even though he couldn't afford much, I always knew he would move mountains and rearrange the stars in some way, shape, form, or fashion if it meant protecting me.

I'll spare ya'll on all of the details, but my dad was able to convince one of his old homeboys from the projects he grew up in to take my case. That brother showed up to the station and showed out. Before they could officially book me into general population, I was a free woman, and they were already talking about dropping the charges on me. It was then that I realized that even though I had been around niggas with money, I had never been around someone with *real* control or authority. The way that man smiled as he articulately clowned those cops for what he called a wrongful arrest got me to reevaluate what I considered to be a *boss*.

1

MARRIED TO THE MONEY

Attorney Jared Brooks made me a free woman in more ways than one the day he got my charges dropped.

For the first time in my life, I didn't feel like I needed to risk my freedom just to have access to the wealth I aspired to have. Instead, I decided that I wanted to find a man who wore a suit like he did. One who could walk and talk himself into or out of anything.

Fast forward to a decade and some change later, I was now a thirty-five-year-old woman in a marriage with a successful attorney. When I met Donnell Bryant, I just knew that we were going to get married one day. Sure, he wasn't rough around the edges like most of the street niggas I had dated before him, but he was sweet, ambitious, and could talk a mean talk. He wasn't as tall or even as fine as the men that I previously dated. Still, he seemed to have a good relationship with his momma and God, and we all know that's a true recipe for a winning relationship, right?

I'm not sure how I managed to neglect his evident love for the attention of other women for so long. Maybe I was just so caught up in how special he would make me feel that I refused to allow myself to see what was right in front of me. Either way, once I noticed it, I was convinced that his actions would eventually land me back in someone's booking station.

Anyway, I didn't need him or anyone else to tell me that I was bad. Shit, I knew that already. No one would ever convince me that my dark complexion was anything less than perfection. After all, my skin complements gold, and any other color for that matter.

Although I wasn't blessed with large, round, perky breasts or the fat ass that seems to be a part of everyone's beauty standard now, my curves were just as dangerous as a woman who had blown through her tax money in Doctor Miami's office. You see, I already know I'm the shit. Whether I'm anyone else's cup of tea or not I will always be confident in myself. Therefore, I don't need a motherfucking soul to validate me or how I feel about myself – ever.

That sounds good, huh? It should because that is how I genuinely viewed myself until a couple of years ago. Halfway into our four-year marriage, I started comparing myself to the women I would find in my husband's phone whenever my suspicions would get the best of me.

What the fuck could they offer that I haven't already given him? Donnell and I had been together since I was twenty-one. That meant that I stuck by him when his ass was just a struggling college student with dreams of being a boss one day. Didn't he know that I suffered through that time too? Hell, I had to momentarily let go of my obsession for expensive things because his ass definitely couldn't afford it. Not only did I have to deal with being broke, but I also made sure to love and encourage his ass throughout the entire process. Wasn't that worth some sort of loyalty?

To add insult to injury, Donnell wasn't even really my type. I had always melted at the sight of a tall, barbaric man who commanded attention when he walked into a room. Donnell's ass is only 5'10. That means that at 5'7, I'm not even allowed to wear the length of heels I want to without my stilettos deflating his short-ass ego.

I know it sounds like I'm just doing a lot of complaining, but can you blame a bitch for being fed up with this bullshit? When I initially started dating as a teenager, I only wanted nice things. Now, as I'm growing older, I'm beginning to realize that having expensive shit is nice. Still, it's not going to sustain me forever. I want a relationship that was built like the ones my parents had. To this day, I've never heard about my daddy stepping out on my mama. In fact, he seems to still worship the ground she walks on. Sometimes it makes me realize that even though our house was small and lacked most of the things the mansion I have now has, it was filled with the one thing this place can't seem to find: love.

Last year, I decided to take a break from my marriage, and I packed up a small suitcase to live with my parents while I figured out what I wanted to do. Because I got married to a man with money, I didn't pursue many of the opportunities in front of me. Can I be transparent for a minute? Up until the last year of my life, I just knew I wanted nice things. I never planned on how I would finance them, so I always prepared myself to just be a good-looking wife with nice taste in stuff.

Being separated from Donnell was easy. It was peaceful not to hear him lie to me every day. I'm no dummy; I'm sure while I was gone, he used the home I once prayed for to entertain his harem of whores, but for the twelve months that I was gone, I didn't give a damn.

I knew I would eventually come home; however, there was something about his persistence to fix our marriage and start over that I started to believe. I guess that's a part of the curse of being with a man who can talk himself into or out of anything. He can talk himself into the drawers of another woman and then turn around and later talk himself out of a divorce with me. Against my better judgment, I moved my small suitcase back home and joined marriage counseling with my husband.

In the beginning, things felt different. He was more attentive to me and seemed to enjoy going out of his way to please me. It felt nice to be desired by the only man I had committed myself to for so long. For a while, I stopped searching for ways to catch him in a lie because he made it so easy to believe he was trustworthy. Well, honey, that moment was over almost as soon as it started.

"I guess I just struggle to be honest in relationships," Donnell confessed during our weekly counseling session. "I love my wife, but I'm struggling to let go of the other women around me. I'm tired of feeling like I'm living a double life."

I sat there in shock as the world around me started crumbling under my feet.

Had the last few months been a lie?

Was I unknowingly cast a role in a Tyler Perry film that I didn't agree to play in?

"I just don't understand why she won't be open to loving me for who I am and not a version of who she wants me to be. I don't plan to be this way forever. Shoot, it sucks to have these desires come over me, but I just don't want to lose my wife and the life we've built in the process."

Yeah, right nigga. You just realize that if I left you that I'm immediately coming for half of everything.

"Truthfully, there is just a handful of women that I've been flirting with for years. I don't think I'll be able to move past this point in my life if I'm not awarded the freedom to put it all behind me," Donnell continued.

Kat, just shut the fuck up. Donnell has been lying and cheating since we met him. He obviously has no immediate plans to change.

I wanted to explode. I could feel the rage surging inside, and everything in me wanted to slap the shit out of him.

Why did he bother making me those promises if he knew he wasn't going to fulfill them? Does this nigga think I'm just a toy he can play with whenever he wants to?

Unable to be silent any longer, I interjected. "Let me get this straight. You expect me to just put my life on hold while you work out your *desires?* Haven't you spent most of your time exploring other women? You would think you would be sick of it at this point." I couldn't hide my disgust. While I realized and understood the rules of engagement on disagreeing in therapy, there was just no way I could avoid that last petty comment.

"Katrina, please," he pleaded as he turned to face me and grabbed my hands. "Remember some years back when you admitted to me about being curious about women yourself?"

Oh, hell no. I know he is not taking an admission I made during our young party years to prove a point. This motherfucker has no shame!

"I didn't judge you for your feelings then. In fact, I encouraged you to explore them. Did I not?"

Yeah. That way, I wouldn't be on your ass about all the women you can't seem to let go of.

"I know you probably think that it would just be an excuse to do me, but I promise it's not like that," Donnell added. "Don't you still think about it every now and then?"

I didn't want to answer his last question because I hate when he's right. Although I never admitted it to him again, I occasionally wonder what it would be like to know another woman intimately. Despite my usual disgust over the confirmation of my husband's infidelity, I found a couple of women to be breathtakingly beautiful. Can I be super honest with ya'll again? There is a woman that seems to consistently flood my husband's phone with videos. I've used a few of the ones I found to get off. I'm not sure what it was exactly. Maybe it was the way her manicured hands rubbed softly on her large breasts and perky nipples. Or perhaps it was the fact that when she slid her fingers in her pussy, you could hear how turned on she was. Either way, it always excited me and made me even more curious than I had been. Regardless, I had always expected my curiosity to be something that was buried in the grave with me. I never had any plans to act on it. Something about him choosing to bring up such a personal secret of mine infuriated me. I know we are in therapy, but he shouldn't have confessed my secrets without talking to me first.

"What the heck, Donnell? Why would you feel the need to bring this up?" I let go of his hand as the embarrassment I was feeling began to overtake me.

Speaking up since the first time my husband started dropping bombs on me, Gabriella, our therapist, tried to ease the tension in the room.

"Katrina, what has you the most upset right now," she asked in a calm tone.

"I don't know. It could be the fact that he always has to manipulate shit with me to try to get his way."

Kat, just shut the fuck up. This isn't going to change anything anyway.

"Do you truly believe your husband was using this moment to exploit you, or is it possible that these feelings may be stemming from something else," Gabriella asked.

I took a moment to respond to her because I already knew where she was leading this conversation. Although I was previously resistant to counseling, Gabriella was great at what she did. We had been to enough sessions that I knew she would remind me that anger was a second-hand emotion that is usually used to mask the real problem.

"I'm just at a point where I only want my husband. I've been using my sexuality to get what I want since I was a teenager. Now, I just want to explore my sexuality with my husband only. It's hard to imagine that the man I love and have committed myself to be with can't seem to want me in the same way," I responded.

"Thank you for sharing that," Gabriella stated. "Donnell, what do you have to say in response to your wife's vulnerability?"

"That's the thing, Kat. I don't want these other women the same way I want you. When I think of spoiling someone — it's only you that I think of. When I think of growing old and traveling the world or playing with our future grandkids, I think of only you. No other woman could ever take your place.

My desire to try new women from time to time does not diminish my love and feelings for you.

In fact, if it would make you feel better, why don't I give you the transparency you deserve by being 100% honest with you on the women I think I need to get out of my system. In return, we can try them out together. You explore a part of you that you've tried to ignore, and I'll put this shit behind me. We can lay down some ground rules, and we can agree that we only do it with the women you approve of. You've gone through my phone hundreds of times. Surely, there was a woman that sparked your interest at least once.

What do you say?"

<u>2</u>

STARTING OVER - AGAIN

Despite my husband's obvious transparency, I couldn't bring myself to admit the truth. Had I thought of some of the women that I saw in his phone previously? Sure, I have. Have I ever wondered if their breasts were as soft as they looked or if they tasted just as sweet as I imagined? Of course, but I was still processing my sexuality myself, and I just wasn't ready to admit it in front of two other people.

Adding to my internal conflict was the spiritual journey I was on with my husband. When we agreed to restore our marriage, we did it under the agreement that we would keep God first and foremost by following His foundation for marriage. After all, a marriage is supposed to be a three-fold chord with just the husband, wife, and Holy Spirit, so how the hell would random people fit into this equation?

It had been a few days since our conversation in therapy, and we were both tiptoeing around the mansion as we avoided the massive elephant in the room.

I didn't know how to break the ice, but I knew he was waiting on me.

"Donnell," I called out sweetly as I caught him on the way to the kitchen. "Do you think that we could get close tonight? I've really been missing you."

Even though we have been together for so many years, I never really know how to initiate sex with my husband unless I'm drunk. In the beginning, it wasn't like that. I thought I knew how to turn him on and how to excite him in the bedroom. Then, I found the messages of all the kinky shit he was into, and it made me second guess everything I was doing.

The Succubus, as I've jokingly called the woman I can't stop thinking about, has a magical way about her. It makes it easy to see why my husband refuses to let go of her, even at the threat of losing his marriage. Her ability to suck a man whole is hypnotizing, and the way she glares into the camera as she pleases herself makes you want to join in with her.

I think I refuse to admit my attraction to her because she forces me to face the insecurities I have about myself. Yes, I'm confident in how attractive I am. Still, after years of watching other women win my husband's attention effortlessly, I realize there are many things they have that I don't. Like me, The Succubus has rich, chocolate skin. Unlike me, her ass is fat, her boobs are perky and large, and her pussy always seems to be juicy and wet.

Back in the day, when I was using my sexuality to get the things I wanted, I never actually had sex with the men I enticed. Because truthfully, most men don't care about how good it is. A lot of them just want to try something new. I played on my innocence, and the men I attracted ate it all up.

Shit, that was the part Donnell loved the most about me in the beginning. He loved that I was willing to try whatever – at least once because I hadn't tried much. Then, once I started finding all the other women he was also experimenting with, I would always respond with, "Go ask one of your other bitches." Even though that was the last thing I wanted him to do.

I waited for a moment as the silence in our home seemed to last forever.

"Katrina, if you want sex then you know you can initiate it by offering me a back massage or foot rub. I don't know why you insist on initiating it like this when you have the choice to help put me in the mood." Without even bothering to look at me, he continued what he was doing.

What? At that moment, I just wanted to scream. Why did I need to *put him in the mood*, yet he always seemed ready to go for these other bitches he was fucking with? I know good and damn well none of those hoes are putting in work for penis, so why should I?

Instead of greeting him with the hostility that was brewing deep inside of me, I took a deep breath and tried to mask my annoyance.

"Help me understand this, Donnell. As your wife, you need me to help you desire me for sex; however, other women can do it without any effort at all? Can you please make it make sense because I clearly don't get it.?"

"Katrina, you've been giving me pussy for years. It's the same thing every time. With them, I'm just ready to go because it's exciting to try something new. Some of these women are a little more experienced, or they're willing to try things that I just don't have the patience to teach you," he yelled out casually from the kitchen.

In that moment, a million things ran through my mind that I could have and should have said to him. But at times like this, I remind myself of those ice-cold cuffs, and it helps bring me back to a better mental place.

Kat, just shut the fuck up. It's not going to matter what you have to say anyway.

"Look baby," he said as he walked out of the kitchen with a plate of food that I slaved over making for him. "I wish you wouldn't make it such a personal thing. You're beautiful but look at it like this. I love when you cook for me. I loved it so much that I made the decision to marry you so that I could have access to it forever. Regardless of how much I love your cooking, I still like eating out at other places. Does that mean I love your food any less? Hell no, but I just need to try some different things every now and then. One day I might want a little sazón and Latin spices. Then, on another day, I may desire Chinese food or Italian food, but nothing will ever replace this good ol' home cooking that I have access to whenever I want."

Leave it to a lawyer to find some fucking way to make his point even if it sounds dumb as hell.

"I'm confused baby," Donnell said as he started talking again. "You asked for honesty, right? Didn't you want a marriage where we were free to be ourselves? Instead of being so worried about me and what I desire, why don't you consider what it is that you feel you really need or want?"

The Succubus immediately came to my mind.

I'm not sure if it was his obvious attempt to turn the conversation from me being horny and wanting him or if it was if it was the thought of her tongue on my body, but I was suddenly not interested in him touching me anymore.

Truthfully, I wanted to try new things, but what the hell do I look like sharing my husband with a woman who may have a desire to take my place? Shit, I don't want to think about him being with another woman like he is with me. I don't even want a woman looking at him too long. Why doesn't he understand that? I know he would lose his mind if he had to share me with anyone else. Why is he allowed to do something that I'm not?

I stood there, in silence, as he justified his emotions for wanting more women than me. He was basically admitting a thought that has haunted me for most of our marriage. I, Katrina Bryant, would never be enough for the man I married and gave my life to.

It didn't matter if I had sex with him every minute of every day. Matter of fact, I could suck dick until my lips stayed entrenched in that position for the rest of my life. I could learn to cook Chinese, Latin, or whatever meal he was in the mood for that day. I could even agree to letting a bitch eat me out while he drilled that part of him that was supposed to be reserved for me — into a new woman every day of the week. No matter what I scarified, whether physical or emotional, he was always going to want someone else.

I watched his mouth move as that heavy realization took root in my heart.

Which hand should I slap him with?

If I cried, would he at least attempt to see things my way?

Is this how I would live my life forever if I stayed married to him?

How far is he willing to go with this lifestyle? I've seen videos online about all of these new relationship types.

Was he trying to make me wife number one?

How many fucking bitches would this nigga truly need?

Indisputably, I could have stood there all day, stuck in that trance of countless thoughts. My *husband* was literally blind to the unmistakable pain on my face. He was too busy going on and on about his different fantasies. It's like he didn't give a damn about how heavy his truth could have been for me.

If I smacked the fuck out of him, would he call the police on me?

Damn, would that make me an abuser?

Obviously, I know I can't beat his ass up. I just feel like he needs to feel the pain he's literally putting on me.

Would his ass, hit me back?

What if I didn't say anything? Would he think that everything was good with us?

I wanted to jump out of the rabbit hole my mind was in, but I couldn't. Why the hell did it take me so long to accept the shit he's been showing me since we first got together? I've caught him cheating a number of times; yet, I really thought he would change.

For the first time in years, I heard my husband loud and clear. In fact, I could *truly* see him for who he was and not who I desperately wanted him to be for me.

How would he feel if I decided to play into his game? I mean, at this point, it's either join in or get the hell off the bus, right?

"So let me get this straight," I interjected. Surprised at my sudden inability to keep my thoughts to myself. "You want to open up our marriage?"

He didn't immediately agree. Of course, the lawyer in him had to dance around my direct question.

Again, I interjected.

"That's not what I asked you, Donnell. Are we going to agree to opening our marriage? It's a direct question. I'm not sure why you're having a hard time answering it."

"Come on, Kat. What nigga wants his wife getting dug out by another man? Is that what you want to do now," he asked.

Is he jealous? I know this isn't the same nigga that was just pouring out all his desires trying to stifle my ideas.

"Maybe," I responded nonchalantly. "I mean if we are opening that door, I might want to try it down the line. Why would you be the only one to get something out of this?"

For the first time in a long time, Donnell was speechless.

That rarely happens.

His eerie silence made this moment even more dreadful.

When he finally spoke up, his low, even tone made it difficult to tell what emotion he was truly feeling.

"Kat, you want to fuck with other niggas? Don't I give you everything? Don't you see that I'm working through this phase in my life? How am I ever supposed to get past this phase if you're out here worrying about some other niggas dick instead of the shit you're supposed to do around here."

Now, it was my turn to sit there, in a sea full of emotions, silently calculating my response.

Truthfully, I just want my husband to only want me. If that were possible, I would be okay with not experimenting with other people.

Sadly, that just wasn't the reality I was living in. Now, I can either continue to put myself in situations to have my feelings crushed or I could just accept him for everything he is.

"I want you and only you. As crazy as it sounds, in my mind, I like to imagine a time when you gush over me the way you do with these women that you refuse to let go of," I started. Against my better judgement, I chose to be honest with him.

"Do you have any idea what it feels like to know that you can claim to love me. Yet, your love isn't strong enough to let go of someone whose presence irritates my soul. You don't. Because in the time that we've been together, I barely even look at other guys.

I'm not going to say I'm trying to go get fucked tomorrow, but I'm saying if you get to have your cake and eat it too, then pass some this way and hand me the ice cream while you're at it."

Donnell just stood there, motionless, as he held his plate of food. It was still difficult to make out what emotions he was feeling in that moment.

"I just don't know why you would want another man, Katrina. We've been together all these years, and you've never, ever insinuated wanting someone else.

Have you been fucking people behind my back and not telling me?" He asked.

"Nigga, I'm not you," I wanted to shout back at him. But I was really trying to keep the lessons I learned in therapy. Even though this moment was making that choice almost impossible.

"No, Donnell," I responded flatly. "I've never been with anyone but you in the time that we've been together. I just don't understand how you seem so shocked about me doing the exact same thing that you're doing."

He instantly shouted back, "Because you've always known that I love different pussy. I've never hidden that from you. I might have lied to keep you from leaving me a few times, but it's always been in your face.

You're the one who keeps taking me back.

I hate how it's like you always want to focus on just the negative things that I've done. Can't you see everything else?"

I stood there – stunned – by his bold confessions and question.

During my therapy sessions, our therapist pointed out that I avoid conflict. Apparently, it has a lot to do with the fact that I never really saw my parents argue. Anyway, if you combine that with having first-hand knowledge of jail life, maybe you can understand why I might be more cautious than most. In the hood, they would call me, "scary," and I would agree just to avoid the disagreement. That's why I don't usually combat my husband's stupidity. Typically, I'll find a way to say what I want to say. For some reason, in this moment, I didn't feel that way.

"Donnell, before I allow you to sit up there and insult my intelligence any longer, I'm going to stop you here.

I just think it's funny how you've basically put me in a place where you just expect me to accept the behavior that's caused so many issues throughout the existence of our marriage! Most of our fights are about infidelity and your inability to set boundaries with anything that has a vagina and cute face. Now, you just want me to be ok with it? That's how you really expect this to work?"

"I just want you to love me for me and get through this time with me. Why is that so hard if you say that you love me," Donnell asked.

Ha! No, he didn't try that with me.

Kat, just shut the fuck up. Please. Let's leave it alone before it gets out of hand

"No! If you loved me, you would stop inserting other women into our lives," I shot back, unable to hide my pain. You bring these women in and empower them to feel important to you in some way. I'm your freaking wife! Why is that so hard for you to understand?

It's bad enough that I have to live a dull love life without having to be disrespected by some of the women that you've chosen to shove your dick into.

At this point, forget I asked about sex and just go on with your normal routine," I spat out.

"Ok Kat. You always want to say some petty shit like that, but I bet you would lose your mind if I did it for real.

I'm going to leave my phone open. Find a woman you want to try with me. I'm not asking you anymore. This is what I want to do, and you can join me or not. It's up to you.

Make a decision."

***

"Let me get this straight," The Succubus started as she put down her menu. "You actually want me to join you and your husband in the bedroom. That's why you've invited me here today?"

Now, before you start thinking some crazy shit – hear me out. No, I'm not just doing whatever Donnell says. Truthfully, after I finally accepted the fact that I was not going to be enough for my husband by myself, I started to really consider the idea of being with someone else.

At this point, I want all the attention that other people are receiving and if my husband isn't going to give it to me – then I want to find someone that will. I guess it also doesn't help that there is a part of me that is curious about this woman. I had to find out why. That's why one day I made the decision to just call her and invite her to lunch. Obviously, Donnell didn't oblige or ask too many questions. I think he believes he's finally going to get what he wants. However, this for me, was never about trying to fix my marriage. I wanted to discover a side of myself that I had been neglecting forever.

"I'm just being honest," she continued. "You don't give me that vibe. Like, at all. So, what's the *real* reason I'm here tonight," The Succubus asked.

I wanted to be an open book and share with her my thoughts, but I couldn't do it.

"My husband really thinks that it will spice the marriage up a little bit, so I'm willing to try it," I lied.

She took a sip of her red wine, and then she sat back in her chair. Believe it or not, she looked even better in person. Her pictures didn't do her enough justice.

"What sexual fantasies will you be living out," The Succubus asked.

I was caught off guard by her question. I wasn't expecting her to ask me that.

As if she could sense me tensing up, she took her right leg and ran it against mine.

"Katrina, what fantasies will you be living out if I decided to join you and your husband in bed?"

I looked around to make sure no one was watching us before I responded.

"I find you really attractive," I declared as I awkwardly avoided eye contact. "Anyway, my husband has had years to explore his sexuality, and now I think it's my time."

The Succubus sat up.

"And what do you want to do during this new time in your life," she asked seductively.

I sheepishly looked around to make sure no one was paying attention to us.

"I feel like I need a level of intimacy that my husband can't give me. I need something more."

She lowered her leg and adjusted herself in her seat.

"Listen, I enjoy being a comet and the threesomes I have because of it, but I have to be real with you. Bringing another person into your bedroom isn't going to fix your issues – it's going to amplify them. If you have an issue with the intimacy you're getting from your husband, do you think watching him fuck someone else is going to make that go away?"

"I don't want to try to fix the intimacy with him anymore. I want to try it with someone else. I'm open to experimenting, but I don't know if I want it to be with him," I responded.

"Oh," she replied as she picked up her wine glass and took another sip. "I guess that makes things a little messier then, huh? Now that the cat is out of the bag, can I finally have the truth? Why did you invite me here?"

Damn. I thought to myself. *I was hoping my previous answers were enough to satisfy her curiosity.*

I looked around again. Only this time, she leaned forward and placed her hand on mine.

"Katrina, why do you give a single fuck what anyone in this restaurant has to think? You're a grown woman and you deserve to be pleasured. Don't you agree?"

"Well, obviously," I started before she interjected.

"Then start owning your shit. Stop living your life to please others. You're just as responsible for your nut as the person sharing the bed with you. That innocent crap only worked when we were kids. Now, you'll get more by demanding what you want and nothing less," The Succubus stated.

I didn't expect her to give me a lecture, but I was glad to have her company. I missed having homegirls. Throughout the years, I had just grown paranoid that the ladies I brought around wanted my husband or vice versa. That made it hard to maintain anything that even looked like a possible friendship.

"Do you see that guy across the room at the bar," she asked –

breaking the trance I was in. He's wearing the black and red polo shirt."

I turned my head to scan the room. The moment I saw him, I quickly looked away.

"Girl! What did we just say about owning your shit? I've lost count of how many times I've seen that man glance over here to admire you. You should send a drink his way. Better yet, you should walk over there and buy him one."

Is this girl drunk already? There is no way I could ever approach a man like that.

I opened my mouth to give her some sort of excuse. As if she could sense it, she stopped me first.

"Do you want to enjoy your sex life, or are you going to continue begging Donnell to give it to you?"

Truthfully, her comment stung. *Had he told her how I was in bed?* I knew coming into this I was going to end up finding out more about Donnell. I really thought I wasn't going to be bothered by it.

"How do you know that I've begged him to give me what I want?" My demeanor changed, and I know she sensed it.

Instead of a feisty, smart remark like I anticipated, The Succubus just chuckled.

"No, Katrina. Your husband has never uttered a word about you personally. I knew he was married, and that was all I ever cared to know. I specifically chose those words to get a rise out of you.

In case no one has ever told you, it seems like you're either timid or rigid. Aren't you tired of being like that?"

This woman – whose name I don't even know, was suddenly reading me like I was last week's newspaper or something.

"Girl, take whatever energy you are on right now and go buy that man a drink," she spoke up.

Right then, my mind started racing with a million thoughts.

Am I doing the right thing?

Is this woman lying to me? Has my husband been trash talking me to a woman that he's been sleeping with?

Is there any truth to what she just said?

How am I ever going to get what I'm searching for if I'm too afraid to step out like Donnell does so freely?

Realizing that last thought was petty, it brought me back to reality.

"What if he rejects my advances," I asked her, forcing myself to be present and at least try to go with the flow.

"Then, he rejects you. You'll live."

I wish it were that simple. There is something about the thought of rejection that keeps me crippled and afraid to do the things I really want.

"Katrina, walk over there, and do whatever you think I would do. If you go over there with a certain sense of confidence, he is going to do one of two things. He is either going to sweat you or he's going to cower. Either one works out in your favor. With all the pent-up frustration you're feeling, you need a beast right now.

Instead of looking at it like he could reject you, just consider the fact that you are vetting out your next intimate partner. Weak men don't deserve your time, much less to be awarded the chance to play inside of your pussy."

I liked the way she thought, and for a moment, I really thought I could do it.

"How should I open…" I started before she spoke up.

"Do I have to drink the water for you too? I led you to the fucking river.

I don't know. Maybe make a comment about his shoes or make a bold statement, but for crying out loud - just go."

Without another word, I stood up from the table and sashayed over to the beautiful black man that was sitting alone at the bar.

What am I doing?

Is this walk sexy or do I look like a newborn giraffe?

Wow. He's cute. I hope my breath doesn't stink.

Oh, God. Please don't let there be anything on my teeth.

Kat, just shut the fuck up. You're doing the best you can. Just chill.

The journey over to him felt like I was walking the death row. In all of my years, I had never approached a man first.

"So did you have plans of coming over to introduce yourself, or were you just going to stare at me all night?" I stated as I sat down without asking for an invitation.

"Are you always this forward," the man asked as he locked eyes with me for the first time since I approached him.

NO! That's the reason why everything on my body is sweating at this moment. I really hope I don't smell weird.

"Truthfully, no. I'm not usually this forward. I just saw a good-looking man that seemed to be admiring me, so I figured I would shoot my shot. Is it working?"

"Yes," he replied frankly. "I'm Mike. What's your name?"

"Katrina," I purred back.

I sat there for a moment while he explained that he was a marketing consultant. Sitting in his presence made it easy to see how he could be successful in business. His fine ass had a set of eyes that could hypnotize you. Then, his deep, low voice forced you to draw yourself closer into him. If it wasn't for The Succubus, I would have let that man talk me right out of my panties. She held her watch up as if to tell me to wrap up the conversation.

I pulled out my phone, unlocked it, and slid it to Mike. "Give me your number, and I'll call you later."

Mike chuckled, but then he did as he was told.

"Make sure you call me Ms. Katrina," Mike pleaded with a smile.

Bitch. just run back to the table.

I would look crazy if I did that, huh?

For some reason, I think he was actually feeling me.

I've never felt so confident and powerful in my life!

Damn. Mike is the first man I've truly ever admired or flirted with since being married to Donnell. Should I be worried about how much I just enjoyed myself?

"Bravo," The Succubus declared as I took my seat. "It looks like you can be confident and go after the pleasure you deserve at the time after all. How do you feel?"

The energy coursing through my body felt dangerously powerful, and I liked it.

"I feel great." I said smugly.

"Fantastic. So then, let me ask you again. What sexual fantasies will you be living out during this new experimental time in your life?"

"For a while I've wanted to know how the juices in your pussy taste," I responded back.

As the words were coming up, I could feel my stomach knotting up. Regardless, the energy that was flowing through me was too strong to try to hide or deny my feelings.

"Now, after experiencing that thrill, I want to know what it feels like to test the waters with other men," I continued.

"Good. You deserve to be pleasured too. Donnell is a very selfish lover. He does just enough to get you in the mood, and then before you can fully bust a nut, he's finished."

The Succubus wasn't wrong. Even though I'm inexperienced,

something inside of me knew that there had to be bigger and better pipe layers than my husband.

I didn't respond to the comment she made about Donnell. Truthfully, I wasn't sure what to say. My husband's mistress thinks he's terrible in bed.

Why the hell have I been so jealous about this for so long?

"Make him wait it out a day or two. Then, text him in the middle of the night to ask him what he's doing. After he replies, don't send him another message until the morning. Tell him you fell asleep or something. Guys like him enjoy a little chase.

In the meantime, you need to figure out what pleasure looks like to you. Watch a few pornos while you play with yourself. Gone are the days where you just lay there while someone uses your body to fulfill their needs. Now, you're going to know what you want, and you're going to demand that the men that share your bed with you give it to you."

The thought of playing the dating game felt exciting. Even though he was sitting down, I could tell that Mike had to be tall. He was handsome and seemed to easily carry a conversation. Shit, let me be real with ya'll for a moment. Mike's lips looked so delicious. Between admiring his white teeth and imagining how soft his lips were, I couldn't focus on much of anything else.

I want to get fucked right now. I thought to myself as my pussy got wet.

Why do I have to wait when I know I want to try him tonight?

Since I was forward, will she let me enjoy her without Donnell around?

Damn. Donnell. He still has no idea how deep I'm trying to take this next phase. Do I continue just going after only what I want? If I did, wouldn't that make me just as selfish as him?

Thinking of my husband immediately deflated the hot air that was brewing around in my head.

"I know it seems childish when you're playing games with something you want but trust me it makes the outcome more exciting. You have homework in the meantime, anyway." The Succubus kept talking, but now I suddenly couldn't stop thinking about Donnell and how this was going to impact our lives.

"What's wrong now, she asked, breaking my train of thought.

"I don't know. One minute I was feeling myself and the idea of being this new free version of myself. Then, I thought about

Donnell, and… now I can't stop thinking about him. Am I doing the right thing here?"

Oh, God. How did I fall so far that I am now asking my husband's mistress to confirm my life's choices?

"I can't tell you what to do," she responded. "I've never been married, but I realize the vows you made to each other. What I can tell you is that Donnell faithfully makes the decision to not honor the promises that he made to you. Now, that doesn't mean that you have to play the same way he is, but girl you only have one life to live. Whenever you make your decision, make sure that truth is the foundation of your decision.

You deserve more than just sitting at home waiting for Donnell to stroll in after doing whatever he has to in order to enjoy the only life he is going to be given."

"That sounds a lot like you think I should do it," I responded back matter-of-factly.

She chuckled before responding. "I guess I can see why you would think that, but I promise you that I know better than to make decisions for what married people should do. I can only speak off the things that I know about your husband."

There was something about her tone that made me want to have a conversation that I swore to myself I wouldn't have.

"Just exactly how long have you known my husband like that," I asked.

"Are we really about to have this conversation," The Succubus replied. "I have no problem answering any of your questions, but I just want to make sure you're not trying to be on any drama because that's not why I agreed to come here."

"You're not the first woman my husband has carried on an affair with, and after the shit he's confessed to me, I know that you won't be the last. It would be pointless to start any drama with anything that you share because it isn't going to change anything anyway."

"Ok girl. I just needed to make sure. A bitch is not trying to mess up her money." She must have noticed the puzzled look on my face because she proceeded with some hard truths. "I met your husband five years ago." She paused to take another sip of wine.

Five years ago? That means he started messing with you around the time that he proposed to me.

"We met at a club. He was out celebrating a huge proposal that had just been accepted or something when one of his friends asked me to give him a dance.

That proposal was supposed to be the happiest day of my life. I didn't realize that it would be the excuse that created an affair that shows no obvious signs of slowing down any time soon.

"You gave him a dance?" I asked as I fumbled around in my seat a little bit.

"At night, I'm a dancer. It allows me to have the money to fund my dreams. Anyway, I met your husband while I was working."

I had so many other questions to ask, but I didn't want to offend her.

Why do I care so much anyway?

This isn't why I came here!

Kat, just shut the fuck up and leave it alone. It's not going to change anything anyway.

"Can you just answer one final question? Why did you choose to maintain an affair with Donnell? How did you guys even start messing around if you were just working?"

"I thought you only had *one* final question," The Succubus responded.

We both giggled for a moment before she continued.

"No, I don't sleep with every guy that I dance for – if that's what you want to know. I chose Donnell, despite his selfish and lazy ways, because he seemed to like listening to me speak. Most guys come into the club and expect me to be their therapist. I play the role because I have bills to pay, but he made me feel something different.

Donnell pays me to just sit and talk to him. Then, he started paying me more to be more available I guess."

For the first time, The Succubus seemed to be a little rattled.

Does this woman have real feelings for my husband? Has this really been more than sex all along?

I didn't know how to proceed with the conversation. I told her I wasn't going to ask any more questions, but now I *needed* to know the truth.

"Do you love him," I spat out eagerly.

She didn't immediately answer my question.

Uh-oh.

I never truly saw this coming.

Sure, I considered the possibility a few times, but now that it is in front of me,

I don't know what to do.

I really thought he and I would somehow work out. In the back of my mind, I really wanted to believe that our marriage could withstand anything.

Is this why he wanted to be so honest about what he wanted sexually from our marriage?

OH, Kat, just shut up and leave it alone. You're going to stress yourself out about all of this.

Remember, this is not the reason that we came here.

But now I just have so many questions.

Have they always had an emotional connection?

Does he love her back?

Is this his way of letting me into their relationship instead of the other way around?

Would he have picked her if I would have said no?

Kat, just shut the fuck up. Slow your thoughts down. Take a deep breath.

"Look, before you jump down the rabbit hole, I want to clear up that I genuinely don't know how I feel about Donnell. He seems like a nice guy overall. Even though he buys me nice things and he takes care of me, I realize my position and I play it. You're the woman that he *actually* wants. That's why it doesn't make any sense for me to feel anything for him."

I heard what she was saying, but her demeanor said something completely different.

Why do I feel sympathy for her?

Am I supposed to feel this way about the feelings my husband's mistress is harboring about him?

I watched as she took another sip of her drink. I wanted to speak up so that I could rid us of that awkward silence that had suddenly joined us on our date, but I wasn't sure what to say.

I glanced over at Mike. To my pleasant surprise, he was already admiring me from his side of the room. I blushed in response.

She wants my husband, and I want that gorgeous man that seems so close but so far away from me.

Maybe this can work out for everyone.

"It's obvious that you feel something for my husband." I said finally speaking up. "There is a part of me that wants to slap the shit out of you, but surprisingly it's a very small part. The rest of me wants you to help me get us what we both want." I paused to take a sip of my drink before I spat out the rest of my plan.

"You can have more time with Donnell, and I'm going to need a little help breaking out of my shell while I try to live out my own fantasies and explore new parts of myself.

What do you say?"

3
GAME TIME

I realize that my actions, to a sane person, might sound a little off the wall, but if I'm honest, I'm desperate.

Yes, I still love my husband. I don't think I could ever deny the passion that still burns inside of me for that man. I have just finally reached a place that I cannot hide my desire to try new things either. For years, I did exactly what a good "saved" wife was supposed to do. I cooked, cleaned, and kept my body in pristine shape for my husband. I wasn't argumentative, and I supported him in every single endeavor that he started, and what was my reward? My husband just basically made the decision to put his dick anywhere he wants whether I like it or not.

After my date with The Succubus, I came home to find my husband hot and ready like a pizza. Was I horny? Of course, but I was in a space that allowed me to accept the fact that what I wanted – I wasn't in the mood to get from Donnell.

Because I had to maintain appearances, I did what we always did. I laid there while he drilled into me for five minutes. Occasionally I would throw an "ooh" or an "ahh" in to let him think I was enjoying myself.

"You deserve to be pleasured, Katrina." I could hear The Succubus' words ringing in my ear as I tried to mentally escape being in that bed with my husband. Just the thought of her in that sequenced mini skirt she was wearing moments ago was enough to get me excited all over again.

"Damn," Donnell gasped as my now excited pussy got wet for him. "There's my baby."

Usually, I would have purred something back like, "Yeah, papa. You know this is all yours," but I truly wasn't in the mood to fake it today.

I thought I was doing a great job at pretending to be present with him. Well, that was until he stopped mid-stroke and looked me dead in my eyes.

"What's going on Katrina. This feels different tonight," Donnell stated.

Shit. Do I tell him the truth, or do I pull a Donnell and lie straight through my teeth?

"Nothing, papa. I'm just trying to wrap my head around all of this. Opening our marriage just feels like a lot sometimes." I was honest. I chose to be completely upfront with my husband. Although I was ready to try new things, a part of me is still grieving the idea of what I prayed my marriage would one day be like. Sometimes when I think I'm losing it, it feels like I've already lost him.

"Oh, baby," Donnell started before he took a moment to gently kiss my lips. Then, my neck. "First, I want to thank you for letting us try something new. But more important than that, I just want to remind you that you are the only woman in the world that I want to spend my life with."

Donnell then started slow grinding as he lowered his head to start sucking on my breasts.

If today were any other day, I would have been in heaven. After all, this is basically the shit I've been asking for. Truthfully, I can't remember the last time he held me so tightly while making love to me so passionately. I wanted to give myself permission to enjoy this moment, but I couldn't get The Succubus out of my head.

Maybe it's the fact that he's basically just paying this bitch to be his girl on the side while he's ignoring me.

NO. Kat, just shut the fuck up. You can't think like that!

Ok.

Maybe it's the way that she would caress her leg on me throughout the night.

Maybe it's the way that my body feels when I think of kissing or tasting her.

Oh, Kat, just shut the fuck up for a minute.

"Damn," Donnell moaned as each stroke grew with intensity. "Tell me the truth, what are you thinking about right now."

"The Succubus," I moaned out.

"Who the hell is that?" He asked as he stopped again.

I was nervous to respond. Sure, he said he wanted to try new things, but who knows what to expect in a situation like this.

"The girl I just went out on a date with." I couldn't help but anxiously laugh at myself.

Donnell erupted in laughter.

"Baby, how did you go out with someone not at least knowing their name? Didn't you guys hang out for a while?" He started laughing again.

I was relieved that it didn't bother him to hear my honesty.

"I like that nickname though. Maybe we can use it as our own little inside thing when we are talking about her," he said softly as he started thrusting his hips again.

"I like that," I purred as he got faster.

"What would you do if she was here right now," he asked.

It was hard to concentrate on answering the question because I was starting to feel more relaxed and aroused by him. Usually, Donnell was a selfish lover, but tonight he decided to play with my clit as he slowly moved his hips in a circular motion. I really like that shit.

I locked eyes with him briefly before he threw his head back and slid deeper into me.

"I would want her sitting on my face," I responded as I began playing with my breast. "I want to know what she tastes like."

Again, he moaned.

"What would you want to do," I asked him.

He slowed down his tempo before locking eyes with me.

"What would you be ok with me doing?"

Thank God I didn't blurt out my first initial thought because it was a petty moment. Instead of going there, I made the choice to enjoy myself.

How often do you get to be this honest with your husband, Kat? Just play along and see where this goes.

"I don't think I'm ready to watch you eat her out or…you know…finish inside of her."

"So, if I wanted to watch both of you suck my dick at the same time, that would be fair game," Donnell asked.

I nodded.

He moaned and started thrusting faster.

"I want to hit her from the back while she eats you out," he spoke out.

"Mm... I would like that," I purred back in response.

"Good," he said flatly. "I'll set it up tomorrow."

We kissed and my usual five minutes with Donnell turned into a two-hour full body workout.

The next morning, however, was awkward. Well, to me at least. Donnell went right back to his usual routine, and I suddenly had a wave of energy over me that I needed to release.

Instead of being timid like I usually would, I decided to go in for a kiss before reaching for his dick.

"Not right now," he responded before my lips could land on his. "I got shit to do."

Ok. It's crazy how you seem so turned on when we were role playing the idea of having another woman in our bed. Now you're too busy? Nigga you own the firm. You can get there whenever you want.

It took me a while to get those thoughts from the forefront of my mind. It's just so confusing how we could share something so passionate a few hours ago and then go right back to our boring and dull routine.

I grabbed my phone to check my emails when I saw a text come in from The Succubus.

"I can't stop thinking about you," the text simply read. Before I put my phone down, another one came through. "Don't forget to do your little homework assignment, by the way. I'll know if you did it not when I see you for lunch later."

Damn.

She wants to see me again.

Already?

Damn!

Is she trying to get freaky later? How else would she be able to tell if I found a porno I liked and watched it until I was sure I came. How could she tell if I took the time to explore my own body to find what I liked sexually?

"Have a good day, Kat," Donnell said flatly as he pulled me away from my thoughts.

I do want to cum, and it would be nice to see what kind of positions the three of us could try.

Wait.

Why am I suddenly thinking like this? Am I really going to have a threesome with my husband and a woman that I know has feelings for him?

This is fucking crazy, right?

But if it's such a bad thing, then why does my pussy throb the way it does when I think about eating her out? I suddenly feel like an animal in heat, and I just want to fuck the moment I think about her.

What's happening to me?

"I'm getting ready to do it now." I typed before struggling to hit the send button.

Girl, this is nuts. You still have time to back out of this thing completely.

Despite my fears, I hit the send anyway.

Almost immediately, she responded back, "Send me a picture. Show me something sexy."

I can't do that! Certainly, that's crossing a boundary, right?

What the hell kind of arrangement do we have? Are we allowed to talk to her whenever we feel like? Are we maintaining our own relationships with this woman? How exactly does this work?

I had so many questions, but I decided to just go with the flow for a change.

Once I was sure that he had left, I went to my phone's private browser, and I typed in "ebony lesbian porn."

In college, I discovered that category. Ever since then, it has been my go-to whenever I decided to please myself.

I scrolled through a few videos before I saw one that I liked. To my surprise, it was a threesome.

I never pay attention to the stories because I could care less. I usually just mute the video and let my toy do its thing. This time, however, I was instructed to pay attention to every little detail.

It started off with the two women just enjoying lunch by the pool. They looked like old friends who were just catching up.

How is this supposed to help empower me sexually? The one with the big ass titties just keeps complaining about how she thinks her husband is cheating on her. If anything, it's making me feel silly as hell for doing all of this shit for my own husband.

"He just ignores me. It's like I'm not even there most days," the big tittied woman complained again.

I rolled my eyes. That comment seemed to sit a little too close to home after the morning I just had.

"You're hard to ignore or forget, Tiff," the beautiful Latina responded back. "I can't ever get you out of my mind."

Suddenly, my pussy started throbbing from her moment of blunt honesty.

Tiff, a blond woman with olive colored skin, acted surprised from the shocking comment the Latina had just made.

I watched on, eagerly, as the two-woman stared at each other waiting for the next one to make the first move.

"What do you think about when you think of me," Tiff asked, finally breaking the silence.

The Latina appeared to get nervous at the thought of answering the question. "I've never been with a woman before, so it's kind of hard for me to explain it," she said timidly. "I can show you if you would like."

The sexy Latina with the small waist and big ass stood up and lifted her dress over her head. The frame underneath the dress was even better than I had imagined.

I slid my fingers down to my now wet sweet spot, as my curiosity grew about how this was about to turn into a threesome.

"Come closer," the Latina spoke up seductively.

Without any fight or argument, the big breasted woman scooted closer to where the Latina was sitting.

"I always think of what it would be like to see you naked. Take off your dress for me."

Without any objection, she lifted her yellow dress over her head and was now standing there completely naked.

After taking a moment to enjoy the beautiful woman in front of her, the sexy Latina leaned forward and went in to kiss the woman with the big breasts. They both seemed to immediately like the attention they were receiving.

"Oh," I moaned out loud as I felt my pussy get excited from watching the women explore each other's bodies.

I moved my fingers faster as the Latina laid the blonde woman down on the picnic blanket they had been eating on.

Damn. I didn't even know I found white women sexy.

How the fuck did this end up under this category?

Focus, Kat. All that matters is you saw this big breasted white woman and you suddenly wondered what she would be like in bed. Maybe you have eyes for more than just The Succubus when it comes to being with a woman.

I threw my head back and allowed myself to enjoy my own body as I listened to the two women sing out their oohs and ahs.

"What the fuck," Asked a man with a deep, raspy voice. His presence in the scene brought me back into the moment as I looked at the screen to find out what was going on.

"Tiff," the man spoke up as he was shocked to find his wife poolside with another woman. "What's going on here?"

Moments before this, the Latina had played the role of a shy woman who was just looking to explore her sexual fantasies. Now, suddenly, she seemed to have a level of confidence that I only knew The Succubus to have.

"Frank, your wife is too beautiful to not get the love that she deserves. Why don't you undress and help me show her just how beautiful and sexy she is?"

Of course, Frank didn't oblige. That man was undressed by the time I blinked my eyes.

Tiff looked nervous. The actress playing her was doing a great job showing what a married woman probably looks like in that exact situation. She looked sexy and horny but confused as fuck all at the same time.

Frank watched on hungrily as the sexy Latina went back to pleasing his wife. Tiff's face couldn't hide the concern she was probably feeling for her husband at that moment, but what the Latina was doing do her body had her incapable of voluntarily moving a muscle.

Frank started playing with himself as he watched on.

Damn his penis is fat and long. I wonder what that would feel like.

Hm.

I like the idea of watching Donnell pleasure himself while me and The Succubus fool around in front of him.

It wasn't long before the Latina noticed and decided to really bring Frank in on the action.

The two ladies came up to their knees and Frank walked over and put his thick dick straight into his wife's mouth. The sexy Latina just stroked them both gently as Tiff went to town on her man.

The look on Frank's face tells me that his wife isn't usually this freaky for him.

Slowly, the Latina started joining in and it was just a matter of time before their tongues were sloppily moving across Frank's penis.

Damn. Donnell said he would love to see us do this.

Again, I put my head back as I really began to enjoy the homework assignment. Seeing other people do it, even if it was a scripted porno, made me feel less foolish for wanting to open our bedroom. In fact, it just showed me how turned on I am at the opportunity to explore myself and someone else.

I felt myself ready to release when the vibration from my phone brought me back to reality.

"Stop playing with yourself and send me a picture." The Succubus requested.

I giggled at her persistence, but I wanted to finish catching this orgasm.

I swiped up to ignore her text message and then went on enjoying the show and playing with myself.

"Hmm…" I moaned out as the three of them took the exact position Donnell said he wanted to see. Tiff laid back while the sexy Latina started eating her out. With her fat ass up in the air, Frank used that as a moment to shove himself inside of her.

Tiff looked like she was having way too much fun to care that her husband was now hip deep in some sexy ass woman.

The thought of doing that with Donnell and The Succubus took me right to the edge of my orgasm.

Then, just before I could finish, I saw that she was calling. I contemplated answering, but I ultimately made the decision to see what was so pressing.

"The goal was never for you to cum," The Succubus said before I could even utter a greeting. "I wanted you to do exactly what you are doing now. I wanted you to get close enough so that everything I do today will torment your body to no end.

Get dressed. I'll pick you up in an hour."

"So," The Succubus started as soon as I was comfortable in her car. "How did your assignment go?"

I rolled my eyes in response to her silly question. Who thoroughly enjoys someone not being able to catch a nut?

"Aw," The Succubus responded. "You're a brat when you're horny. Ya'll are the most fun to play with," she tittered.

"Whatever," I interjected. "What exactly are the plans for today? I'm assuming Donnell reached out to you to set this night of fun up, huh?"

"I have not talked to Donell in a few days," she responded with less enthusiasm than she had just a few moments ago. "Our situation does not include daily or even weekly communication."

Wow.

For a moment I was thoroughly shocked. I guess I just always imagined that my husband put in a lot of work to maintain some of his extramarital relationships.

Should that make me feel better or more concerned that my husband has this kind of impact on people that he doesn't deal with that often.

"I was only asking because he brought it up in bed last night. I thought he reached out to you like he told me he was going to. That's all."

I could feel the awkwardness in the room rising. It's like she had more questions to ask, but maybe she didn't know how to.

"Donnell mentioned me during sex with you," The Succubus asked coyly. "How was that?"

"I was already turned on by our date, so it was pretty sexy to be free enough to be honest with him in bed like that," I stated calmly.

There was something about the way that sexy Latina stood on her feelings instead of cowering in them that I wanted to try to embody in my own life and relationships. Something about that small scene with those three lovers showed me that if I'm going to get the pleasure I deserve, I'm going to have to be a willing participant in the process.

"What had you so turned on," The Succubus asked as she moved her right hand from the steering wheel and placed it on my thigh.

I immediately got turned on.

"I thought about how good you looked in that dress last night and how bad I wanted to take it off of you." I spoke up confidently.

"What would you have done if you would have had me alone," she asked as she moved her hand closer towards the opening of my skirt.

Something about being touched by her just feels so sexy.

Is she going to play with my clit because I need to finish?

Is this really going to be how we get intimate for the first time?

Am I allowed to do this right now?

Am I cheating?

My thoughts had overpowered me in that moment, and before I had a chance to answer, she parked the car.

"Well, here we are," The Succubus said as she moved her hand from where it was just a few moments ago.

Fuck!

That's it?

"Where are we, and what are we doing here," I asked while I did my best to hide the irritation I was feeling.

"Donnell has been bragging about these amazing skills that you have when it comes to styling and fashion, and I just have to put it to good use.

I need you to help me stage one of the homes that I'm getting ready to sell. This could be my first million-dollar home listing, and this commission could change the entire game for me."

Seeing her marvel in her dreams was so cute. She seemed genuinely happy and hopeful about what was potentially coming her way.

"I've never staged a home before," I responded as my nerves seemed to flood with uneasiness.

"That's ok," The Succubus responded. "From what I've been told, you know how to make things look good. I need you to make this house look so good that the next person I bring in this motherfucker wants to close that day. Do you think you can handle that?"

I can handle a lot of things. I just don't want to do this right now. I have a thousand other things I would prefer to be doing…

Trying to maintain my composure so she didn't call me a 'brat' again, I casually responded, "yeah I got you." Even though that was the last thing I wanted to do or say.

Anyway, I figure her dancing must pay her very well. Thanks to her large budget, I got everything I wanted and set up in less than four hours.

"This place looks immaculate," The Succubus declared as she sashayed through the large dining room. "I see Donnell was not playing. You have great taste. It's a little expensive, but it's amazing."

We giggled before I took a moment to admire my work. I couldn't argue with her; she was right. My sense of taste cannot be duplicated or re-created. I'm just that *bitch* when it comes to design or fashion.

"A newlywed couple is going to meet me here tomorrow to look around. I know that with my sales game and your skills, I'm going to sell this house."

Standing there, confidently appreciating all her hard work, had to be the sexiest position I had ever seen anyone in.

She let out a deep sigh before she looked over and locked eyes with me.

"Let's bless this place before I sell it tomorrow," she purred as she began sashaying my way.

No way! I can't have sex with her without Donnell, right?

How the heck is this thing supposed to work.

I want her.

Right now.

But if I act on what my body wants that will make me a hypocrite.

What should I do?

"Call Donnell first. Let's see if he wants to join in." I commanded. For a moment, I was shocked with myself.

I guess I'm really doing this. And not only that, but I'm also doing it with a little extra bass in my chest.

Without any hesitation, The Succubus pulled out her phone, called my husband's number, and put the call on speaker.

"Yeah," Donnell answered dryly, just like he would with me.

"Katrina and I were wondering if you could meet us to help us with something," she asked seductively.

"Oh, is that right," he asked just as calmly as he answered the phone. "You're with my wife, Katrina, right now?"

His demeanor was hard to read. I didn't know if he liked that I had met with her today or not.

"Donnell, I'm standing here, watching your wife Katrina as she admires her home design skills in this mansion that she just staged for me. Can you come dick us down for a job well done, or not?" Even though The Succubus had just put her foot down, her tone never lost its sweetness.

"Send me the address. I'm leaving my office in five," was the last thing my husband sent before he disconnected the line.

So that's it?

This is definitely happening then, right?

I'm going to watch my husband fuck a woman he's been fucking since we became engaged.

Technically this is them allowing me into their relationship.

Kat., just shut the fuck up.

Make a decision.

Right now.

If you are going to go through with this and officially open your marriage and

life to other partners, then stand on it.
  Stop going back and forth.
  What's it going to be?

***

Maybe it was my nerves or maybe my husband was excited about finally getting what he had been asking for. Either way, it felt like he was there in record time.

Who is he going to show some affection to first when he walks in?

I know The Succubus is trying to downplay her feelings for Donnell, but what am I going to do when I see them interacting together.

4

MIND OVER MATTER

If you came over here searching for the details of that first rendezvous, let me save you the trouble. I just couldn't do it.

Sure, watching The Succubus stand there naked was something I had fantasized about, but I had to face the facts. I still have a life with Donnell; one that we would need to figure out once our lust went away. Seeing them together kept my thoughts racing. How could I possibly enjoy anything like that?

To my surprise, my husband wasn't upset or angry about the change of plans. Instead, it forced us to start a much-needed conversation that we had been avoiding.

"Being poly is more than sex," The Succubus stated as she put her clothes back on.

Poly?

What the hell is that?

As if he could sense my curiosity, Donnell asked the question that I was afraid to inquire about.

"What the fuck is poly" he asked as he did his best to avoid watching her get dressed.

"It's a lifestyle," she responded with a smirk. "One that requires a lot of vulnerably, conversation, and honesty if you plan on being with multiple people at one time.

Katrina how does this make you feel," she asked as she took a seat right next to Donnell. "I encourage you to be as transparent as possible."

Are we in fucking therapy right now?

How the hell am I supposed to answer that question?

Truthfully, I was looking forward to the opportunity of tasting you tonight. I just feel nervous about watching you fuck my husband since you have feelings for him.

"I'm fine," I lied as I shrugged my shoulders.

"So, you wouldn't care if I sat closer to him right now," she asked as she placed her left leg on him.

"Why would that bother me," I responded.

Ya'll have been getting close for years. This is just the first time that I actually know about it while it's happening.

Kat, just shut up.

Without another word I watched as The Succubus leaned over and laid her head on his chest.

I bet that's how they've been cuddling up. Now, there are just blatantly doing this shit in my face.

"Katrina, I'm waiting for you to tell me when you've had enough," The Succubus said as she ran her manicured nails down Donnell's shirt.

Why the fuck hasn't he stopped this yet? He has to know that I'm not ok with this shit.

"Baby I thought we both wanted this," Donnell said sweetly. "Why don't you come over here?"

Nigga, why don't you fucking end this shit? Is what I wanted to shout out, but I couldn't bring myself to say a word. Instead, I watched on as my mind threw darts at me.

It doesn't matter what you want, Katrina.

Donnell wants this.

He wants her and she wants him back.

You don't have to play this game anymore.

You can walk away and never have to deal with these motherfuckers again.

People get divorced every day.

You've left before.

This time you would just need to stay gone.

They deserve each other.

Let them be together.

If you speak up, you're going to look like the problem here. Then, they'll just continue this when you're not around.

The Succubus slowly moved her manicured hand down to Donnell's lap.

Bitch, how much more of this do you need to see?

"Are you just going to sit over there," The Succubus asked. "We can have these hard conversations, or you could come join me in pleasing your husband. Either way, I'm going to keep going until you show or tell me what your limits are."

She never once broke her gaze with me as she unbuttoned his pants and pulled out his rock-hard dick.

Stop this, Katrina.

You don't know what you're liable to do if this continues.

She's obviously not going to stop.

Why do I care so much?

Obviously, Donnell doesn't give a fuck about our marriage.

Why can't I just decide to leave his ass alone?

Do I really love him or am I just trying to hold on to the idea of a long marriage like my parents?

Am I happy doing this shit?

Would I be happy if I left him and did my own thing, or would I miss him every day like I did before?

Is this want I want?

The moan that escaped Donnell's mouth when she swallowed him hole was what I needed to finally speak up.

"I just feel like even if we did try to set up some sort of boundaries for whatever this thing is - you guys wouldn't care or follow them," I spat out.

The Succubus sat up while Donnell let out a deep sigh.

Oh, great.

Now, I'm interrupting his nut.

I'm sure this conversation can only go downhill from here.

Just shut the fuck up, Kat.

"A lot of people think being poly is only about the sex. The truth is this kind of dynamic only works when people make the decision to honor and respect other people's boundaries."

The Succubus stopped to wipe the corners of her lips. "Shit. Making multiple relationships work at one time is even harder than just being with one person."

Multiple relationships?

I guess I never stopped to think about what would happen after sex, but I don't know about a relationship.

Is this really what I want to do?

Again, Donnell let out a deep sigh. "Kat, remember when we talked about this? You said you were cool with this if I didn't finish in her or eat her out. Baby, I didn't forget," He said sweetly.

I'm not going to lie. I was shocked that he remembered. For the last few years, it felt like he hasn't been paying much attention to the things that I ask him for.

"Can *Jessica* finish now," he asked with a sly smirk as he squirmed around.

I wanted to laugh. Because he knows that I don't know her name, it made me feel more relaxed in that moment.

Donnell doesn't stop being my husband just because he's with her.

If I decide to be with someone else, it is not going to change the dynamic I have with him.

How the hell did I go from wanting to leave this man to seriously considering this shit?

"Only if you will finish answering some of my questions," I stated as I got comfortable in my seat.

Donnell grabbed the back of The Succubus' head and put it back in his lap.

"Ask me whatever you want, baby," he responded as he laid back and relaxed.

"What kind of relationship are you expecting to have with *Jessica?*" I asked him while I did my best to hold in my laughter.

"What are you ok with," Donnell asked in return.

"What do you want with her," I fired back. "I don't want to speak on anything when I don't know what Jessica wants out of this."

"Then just tell me what you want, Donnell. Why is that so hard," I asked.

"I like the way things have been with us. I don't see why we should change anything," Donnell stated dryly.

I was starting to see why The Succubus was originally hesitant to be open about any feelings she may have had with him. He usually isn't very vulnerable with his feelings.

"Donnell, I know this is probably a weird conversation to have with your wife. But if I have to sit here and watch you enjoy getting your dick sucked by a woman you've been messing with for our entire marriage, then you are going to have this difficult conversation with me.

Do you love her?"

Please don't be a dick with your response, Donnell. I thought to myself. Even though Donnell might not be ready to admit his true feelings, I had already accepted the truth. There is no way that two people could have been together for this long without feeling something for each other.

"I never ever thought about that, Katrina. I love spending time with Jessica, but I love being married to you. I never explored that thought because I never thought I could possibly have you both at the same time."

"Well, now that you know that you can. Do you love her," I asked again.

"I… I … I think so," Donnell finally stated.

I watched on as The Succubus seemed to turn up the intensity of what she was doing.

I could see that Donnell wanted to enjoy it but at the same time he was concerned about how I was feeling.

"I'm sorry," he mouthed to me.

At that moment I felt a sense of freedom that I don't think I've ever felt before. Maybe it was the realization that even though my husband was selfish in some of his desires, it was obvious that he still loves me and considers what I say and need. Maybe it was because I realized that if I wanted a sense of trust to explore a dynamic like this on my own, I was going to have to give it first. I don't know, but I felt like they should have the freedom to explore each other after the confession that my husband just made.

I got up and walked over to where he was sitting and bent over.

"Don't be," I whispered in his ear before I gently kissed his cheek. "Ya'll enjoy your night. Donnell, I'll see you at home." I said before I turned to make my way to the door.

"This convo isn't over," was the last thing I heard Jessica say before I confidently strutted out of there.

I pulled out my phone to order myself an Uber when I thought of my encounter the other night with Mike.

Well, I'm already in the habit of doing a lot of shit that I wouldn't typically do. What's one more wild decision?

Without any more hesitation, I confirmed my car was on the way and decided to spend the rest of my evening getting to know the mystery man from the other night.

5
BO$$ UP

"We spent the entire night just getting to know each other. Mike claims that he is someone that is just well connected and makes things happen," I stated as I finished running my therapist through the last few days of mayhem that my life had turned into.

Jessica did sell the house the next day, and it seemed like after that everything immediately changed for me. Apparently, the young couple were a part of Orlando's most elite socialites, and they told all of their friends and associates about my design skills on their new home. Before the end of the week, I had a booked schedule for the next seven months and I had news stations calling me asking me for interviews. Everyone wanted the chance to tell the breakout story of some unknown stay at home wife who had suddenly become the stylist of the rich and famous.

"Katrina, this story sounds amazing and Mike sounds like a great guy, but I haven't heard you mention Donnell once," Gabriella pointed out as she jotted down a few more notes on her notepad. "How is he taking all of this?"

I didn't immediately answer her question because I honestly wasn't sure how to respond.

Do I tell her about how much time he's been spending with Jessica now that they've both admitted to being in love with each other?

Should I start with telling her that he spent the night out even though that wasn't a part of our original agreement?

And he did it without asking first!

Should I mention that he casually strolled in the next day like everything was all good and then had the nerve to get upset what I asked about it?

Should I tell her that that he tried to make me feel crazy for being upset about his sudden change in plans?

Maybe she wants to know about how Mike has used a lot of his connections to get me contracts with some of the wealthiest people that live on the east coast of the United States? I'm sure it will help her to know that I also spent the night out when I started to see that my husband was moving funny.

Man, how the fuck can I explain to anyone just how much my life has changed in such a short amount of time?

"It's a lot for all of us," is all I could muster up to answer her question. "I don't think he knows how to initiate the conversations that we need to have, and sadly I haven't had much of the time to do it either. As a matter of fact, I'm going to have to change how often I can come to therapy. This is throwing a huge dent in my current schedule."

"Katrina, do you hear yourself," Gabriella responded as she put down her pen and pad. "When we first started this, you were an open book who seemed hell bent on doing anything to fix her marriage. Now, you are complaining about how inconvenient it is. What has changed?"

Me.

I've changed.

I've learned that I can't offer to anyone something I won't give to myself first.

I learned that I'm more than just a wife that stays at home cooking, hoping her husband is in the mood for whatever I cooked that day.

I now know that I don't have to beg someone to give me something when there are other people out there ready to give it.

I'm a boss bitch that is in the process of building my own corporation, and I'm starting to see who is truly there for me.

I'm a new version of myself.

I don't know that Donnell can even identify with this woman, and if you judge from his lack of effort recently, I don't think he has any interest in getting to know this new woman I am.

Shit, I don't even feel like he deserves to be with this version of me.

"Gabriella, throughout this process I've followed your exercises and ideas even when it didn't make sense to me in the moment. I learned to love my husband purely for who he is and not the version of him that I had concocted in my head.

For the first time ever, I feel free. I don't feel the need to restrict who he is. Instead, I embrace the chance to really see how he moves when I'm not there to complain about everything he does. Is there really a problem in that," I asked knowing that if anyone was going to find the problem – it was definitely going to be her.

Gabriella let out a deep sigh and reclined back in her seat before she responded.

"I'm never here to judge you or the life that you decide to live. My mission has always been to help you arrive at this place of freedom where you don't feel like you have to hide behind defense mechanisms or a façade of who you think the world wants you to be.

I, for one, am excited about all these new changes happening for you. You deserve happiness, and like you've mentioned, we've worked on your self-confidence, so I'm glad that you've arrived here.

I just hope that you can see why I would be concerned. This time last month, you were furious at the thought of your husband being with another woman. Now, you are suddenly so nonchalant about everything – even this new relationship that you are in.

How much of this new version is genuinely you, and how much of this is just the child version of you that is afraid to speak up because she feels like what she has to say isn't important enough to be heard or respected?"

***

Gabriella's thought-provoking question tormented me for the rest of the day.

She may be a professional, but she's not perfect.

I know she has her own life that she has to deal with, so how can she possibly have all of the answers for me and my marriage?

I tried to force my mind to think about anything but that damn question she asked, but it felt impossible.

How genuine is this person that I'm claiming to be?

Am I really hiding behind the fear of feeling like people don't care about anything that I have to say?

Thankfully my phone's ringer saved me from fighting those same thoughts for a minute.

"Designs by K. Bryant, this is Katrina speaking," I answered without checking my phone's caller ID.

"It's Jessica," The Succubus stated once I was through with my opening. "We need to talk."

Her words brought a heaviness to my stomach. Even though I wanted to know what she wanted to discuss, I wasn't ready to have any other deep conversations today. Gabriella left me with enough to worry about for the rest of the day.

Just play it cool, girl.

Stay out of your feelings and keep it cordial.

"I'm running late to my next appointment, but I have some time while I'm driving. What's up, love?" I tried to sound as sweet and unbothered as possible.

"Well, for starters, how are you," Jessica asked.

Bitch, you have a lot of nerve.

I give you and Donnell a little freedom to explore these feelings that you two have, and now my husband is spending the night out and planning more date nights for you in a week that he has for me since I decided to give this marriage another try.

I'm feeling like you deserve these hands after I thought you and I were building our own friendship or relationship, and now that you have my husband you only call me when you want to talk.

What about me?

"I'm blessed and highly favored. Business is great. How are you," I asked while I swallowed all my real emotions.

Jessica let out a sigh before she answered. "Truthfully, I've been really confused, and I just want to know how we can get things back to how they were a few weeks ago. I was looking forward to whatever it was that we were building. It's like once you gave Donnell and I your blessing, you didn't have much of a desire to get to know me anymore. Am I right to feel this way?"

Damn. She's direct as hell.

Even with all of this growing, I think that is a quality I want to get better with. I want to have more confidence having harder conversations.

"Oh, it's nothing personal. You know how it is when you are building a business," I lied.

"Of course, I do," Jessica responded back. "That's why I know you're full of shit. Right now, you need tons of help, and yet you haven't said a word on how we can help you."

Did she just say "we" as in her and my husband?

This bitch is even more bold than I could have ever imagined.

"Well, the two of you guys have just been so busy with your sleep overs, I didn't want to bother you guys and this honeymoon you appear to be on."

Fuck. I didn't mean to come in so hot, but there was something triggering about her using the word "we" when talking about the man that I'm still freaking married to.

"I told him that we needed another conversation before just doing that," was all Jessica could say before I hung up the phone.

All of a sudden, this bitch is fluent in French. I've never heard the word "we" used so much until just now.

When my phone starting ringing again, I just *knew* it was her calling back.

"Listen, I don't have time for this sh-," I started to declare boldly before Mike's sexy voice simmered me down.

"It's sounds like you're having a hard day, princess. Anything I can do to make it better?"

Shit. I can think of a handful of things you can do right now to ease this tension I'm feeling.

I giggled. "Oh Mike, you always know just how to re-center me. You calling me right now is just the thing I needed.

How is your day going," I asked trying to shift the tone of the conversation.

Before he could respond, I noticed that I was suddenly getting text messages and phone calls from both Donnell and Jessica.

I guess "we" do everything together now, huh?

Donnell can't even call his wife without his new girlfriend having to be right there with him.

"Kat, are you sure that you are ok" Mike asked as he interrupted my train of thought.

"I'm positive," I lied. "What made you ask me that?"

"Well, I just tried to ask you out two times and it seems like you are everywhere but this conversation."

"I'm so sorry," I responded. "It must just be this area that I'm in. I didn't even hear you. Can you ask one more time?"

"I'd love to know if I can take you out tonight. I heard about this new restaurant on the coast, and I think you would enjoy it."

A coastal date? That means he is taking me out of town for at least one night. That's part of what I need.

I wanted to just give him an answer, but it was becoming impossible to ignore the incessant calls of Donnell and Jessica.

"Mike, can you hold that thought for just ten minutes," I asked him. "I have to take this call. I promise I'll call you back in ten minutes with an answer."

I didn't wait for Mike to respond before I clicked over and answered Donnell's tenth call.

"Yes," I stated dryly.

"Katrina, what the hell is going on with us? Why do I have to blow down your phone now just to get a response from you?"

That's crazy. Did you always expect me to be at home waiting for whatever new request you had for the day?

Was I not meant to go out and live my own life at some point in this marriage?

"Donnell, I realize that you are used to be always waiting for your beck and call, but I do have a new, successful business that I need to tend to. I'm sorry that my day can't revolve around sitting by my phone waiting on you to call," I responded.

We are trying to be bold and direct – not spicy, girl.

Tone it down a little.

"You see, if you didn't just hang up on Jessica after admitting your real feelings, I might have accepted that excuse. Can you stop acting like I don't know you?

What's going on," Donnell asked.

Eight more minutes before I need to give Mike an answer.

"A lot is going on Donnell. I've been busy and you've been busy, so I don't see what the real problem is here. I'm just doing exactly what you do. If you expect me not have an issue with anything, then why can't you give me the same energy that I've been giving you?"

"Katrina, you've never matched my energy. You've always been the bigger person. You've always been the one willing to put in the work to fix us or for us to learn to communicate better. I don't know how to respond to this type of energy from you because I'm not used to getting it," Donnell stated.

Of course.

You expected me to always be that person that was desperate for a relationship, huh? Did you not think that I could one day be the woman that I'm now stepping into?

Donnell didn't wait for me to respond to what he said before he continued talking again. By his third mention of the word "we" I was ready to check out again.

Six minutes before I have to give Mike an answer to his question.

I can finish this meeting and be packed and ready for the road before Donnell has a chance to get off work and get home.

Maybe this is what I need to do.

I know just disappearing and avoiding these conversations with Donnell and Jessica aren't really helping anything, but I have too much going on to let them weigh me down with their feelings when mine don't seem to matter to them anyway.

Then, it hit me.

Right there, stuck between running from my problems and facing them, I was confronted with the hard truth.

Girl, you are not embracing some new version of yourself. You are just running from the inevitable. You are worried that if you slow down right now you will have to sit with the disappointment, hurt, and rejection you are feeling. Running a mile a minute keeps you from having to feel that shit.

Mike, as fine as he is, is nothing more than a beautiful distraction. He showers you in flowers and compliments and you engage with it so that you don't have to deal with the facts.

If you call Mike and tell him yes for tonight. These problems are still going to be waiting on you when you get home tomorrow.

"Katrina," Donnell shouted as he snapped me back to reality. "I miss you, baby. Can we talk this thing out or something?"

Three minutes, Kat.

What are you going to do?

Are you going to keep hiding your true emotions and feelings from yourself and those around you or are you ready to finally boss up and go after everything you deserve?

6

WHO'S THE BOSS ANYWAY?

Watching the sunset over the ocean waters was just the distraction I needed.

"Dinner next to the ocean is such a nice move, Mike. Thank you," I started as I moved some of my mashed potatoes around on my plate. "I guess I should have asked before we left, but I was shocked when I found out that the place we were going was four hours away. You know that I have a lot going on right now, so it's just... I don't know. I just can't..."

Before I could finish my statement, Mike interjected.

"I'm confused. Are you happy with the date or did I try too hard with this move," Mike asked boldly.

I seem to surround myself with people who have no problem being assertive and direct.

Why can't I do the same thing?

"The date is perfect," I responded. "Next time do you think you can warn me that I need to block out at least eight hours of drive time? That would have been nice to know in advance. That's all I'm trying to say."

"Wow," he stated before he took a sip from his water. "I think I'm blown away by how difficult it is to communicate with you. Are you doing this on purpose? Is this meant to be a part of your mysterious charm?"

What the fuck is this guy even talking about? The only mystery here is how did this go from me talking about what I needed to his issues with the way I communicate?

"Katrina, I've been trying to get you alone since the night I met you. For weeks, I just sat back and left myself open for whatever your schedule was.

I get it. You're a wife whose career was just recently shoved into the limelight. You've got a lot going on, and for that reason I haven't pressed you at all. Instead, I listened out for any gaps in your schedule that I could insert myself into. I was intentional about this because I would never want to interfere with what you are building.

In all the time that we've been talking, you've never filled me in with your boundaries and what part I can play in your life. I guess I just wanted to test the waters to see how far we could go before your hubby would have an issue with it."

That's the first time he's ever brought up Donnell.

He's never done that. Not even when I told him I was married.

Does he have more questions about my situation that he's afraid to ask?

"My 'hubby' isn't the one that has an issue with what happened today. It's me," I responded. "Next time, please just give me a heads up.

I think it's sweet that you paid attention to my schedule to plan this, but you also need to consider what I need."

Mike dropped his fork and used his napkin to wipe his mouth. I'm not sure how I did it, but it was obvious that something I said had upset him.

"While we are on the subject of things that you *need*, are you aware of what those things may be," he asked.

He has a lot of nerve.

Of course, I do.

"I'm a grown ass woman, Mike. I know exactly what the hell I need," I responded.

"If that is true, then why did I listen to you complain for weeks about wanting to get away and have a chance to reset. Now that I have you in the closest thing to paradise that your schedule will allow, you are finding something else to complain about?

What's the real problem here? Is this going to cause issues at home," he asked as he hinted about my marriage again.

"Mike, do you have an issue with me being married? It's weird to hear you mention my 'home life' or my 'hubby' because you don't usually care to discuss those things."

"That a lie," Mike replied. "*You* don't like to discuss those things. In fact, I'm starting to see that you don't like to discuss a lot of things.

It's almost like you just expect me to sit around waiting for whenever you want me to fulfill whatever relational needs you have for the day. I asked you if you were aware of those needs because it seems to change every freaking day.

At this point, I'm convinced that you don'tt know what you want, and I'm exhausted with trying to figure it out."

I wanted to run. I wanted to throw my fork down, kick off my up heels and take off. However, because I was four hours away from home that meant that I was going to have to wait this one out like a big girl.

You can always rent a car.

Shit, you can catch a bus.

No.

All of that is just way too dramatic. If I do that, it will raise a whole lot of unnecessary flags.

I can get my own room for the night that way I won't have to talk to or deal with Mike.

This is all getting to be way too much.

I watched as Mike waved down the waiter for our check.

How is this space with Mike also tainted?

For the last few weeks this man has been my safe space. A place where I've felt seen, heard, honored, and respected without having to ask or beg for it. This man has even gone out of his way to help me build my career.

Why am I suddenly so cold towards him emotionally?

Katrina, girl, we've got to start somewhere with this communication problem that we have. We might as well start right here, right now.

"Truthfully, I've been dodging conversations about my marriage because I'm not sure how to answer a lot of the questions you probably have. This is brand new territory for me.

Donnell, my husband, and I recently decided to explore more in our marriage when I finally accepted the fact that my husband just loves being with other women.

Now, before you say any slick comments. I don't look at him any different for how he lives his life. It's part of the reason that I have this freedom to be here with you."

With a small grin, Mike put his hands together for a soft golf clap.

"Good girl. You should really be proud of yourself for opening up like that. I didn't even know that you had that in you," he chuckled.

Maybe it was my vulnerability or maybe it was the fact that I had finally relaxed my nerves for the night, but everything about Mike was suddenly irresistible to me.

Mike's dark brown complexion complimented the crisp white button-down shirt that he was wearing. His full lips looked so soft, I just wanted to lean over and kiss him right then and there.

Mike was speaking about something, but all I could focus in on were the features I had been too busy to see earlier.

Since I met Mike, we've done a lot of talking, texting, and sexting, but that is as far as this connection has gone. Even though I did allow myself to fall asleep in his bed one night as revenge for Donnell staying out, I never had sex with him. Now, suddenly it was all I could think of.

Girl, he really has gone out of his way to help you with anything that you've needed. Who would have known that a nigga you just met would have been willing to apply so much pressure when it comes to you?

In all our sexting, he never sent me a single dick picture. I wonder if it's true what they say about tall, skinny, men.

"I need you to fuck me tonight," I boldly declared.

Bitch. Did you think this through?

What about Donnell and the conversations that you are dodging back home? Do you really think it is a good idea to complicate these things with another sexual partner?

What about the revelation that we just had about Mike possibly being a distraction to my problems?

"Why do we have to wait for tonight," Mike asked as he leaned in closer. "I'm sure I could give you what you want in one of these bathrooms in here."

My pussy immediately started throbbing at the thought of him doing some of the things that he talked about.

Public bathroom sex in this fancy ass restaurant? Bitch that sounds fun as hell. Flirt back and see how serious he is.

"I've never had sex in a public place before," I confessed as I rubbed my leg over his. "What if we get caught?"

"If you do what I tell you to, and you promise to keep your moans down, I'll make sure you won't." The confidence dripping from Mike's voice turned me on even more.

"Get up and go find the bathroom that you want to be fucked in," Mike continued. "When I find you, just make sure that you have those pretty panties off and that dress hiked up. Do you understand?"

"Yes sir," I purred as I stood up.

You're taking this too far, Katrina. What are you going to do if you get caught? That will be embarrassing as fuck if a police officer calls to explain this to your husband.

Donnell is not going to find out about this. He's been having his fun for years. Now, it's my turn.

It didn't take me long to find the restaurants bathrooms. Luckily for me, this place had a family bathroom that was overly spacious and clean.

This is not going to help your problems, Katrina. If anything, this is just going to make everything worse. What if Mike is really packing and puts some shit down on you that you've never experienced before? Are you going to be ready to deal with those kinds of emotions?

Despite the war waging on in my mind, I was ready to get fucked by Mike. For the first time in years, I was free to do whatever I wanted to, and I didn't want to take another moment to consider the consequences.

At this point in the night, I had lost count at how many times Jessica and Donnell had called me. I realized that they wanted to talk but talking was the last thing I wanted to do.

I slid off my panties and placed them in my clutch purse. Then, I lifted my dress above my hips and waited for Mike to come and find me.

It only took a minute before I heard his voice on the other side of the door.

"Are you ok in here, sweetheart," Mike asked before walking in. Once he was safely inside, he closed the door and locked it.

"Damn that dress looks even better when I can see everything that you've been hiding underneath it," Mike whispered as he made his way over to where I was standing.

The next thing I know, Mike lifted me off the ground. I wrapped my legs around his hips, eager for what was coming next.

Savagely, Mike started kissing my neck while his hands explored every square inch of my body. "I can't wait to be inside of you," Mike stated as he pushed my back against the cold wall so he could take his pants off.

You can't let this man go in raw, Katrina! What if you get pregnant? You and Donnell haven't even discussed what his boundaries were.

You can't do this.

My rational mind wanted to stop Mike, but my body was not ready to put up a fight.

I deserve to be fucked like this. I deserve to be admired so much that a man is willing to devour me anywhere I want him to.

What is the problem with me finally enjoying my life?

With one hand, Mike held my body close to his while he used his other hand to rub his large, hard dick against my warm wet pussy.

What they say about tall, skinny niggas is definitely true, I thought to myself as I eagerly waited for him to enter me.

"Hmm," I moaned out unable to contain my desire to have him inside of me.

"Put it in," I demanded.

"How bad do you want it," Mike asked me while he started to increase the speed of his movements.

"I need you inside of me right now," I purred back.

"Grab it and put it in then," Mike stated as he used his other hand to grab me more securely.

Without a fight, I did exactly as he told me to do.

Bitch, you are straight tripping. Have you lost your rabbit ass mind? What if Donnell did this exact same thing with Jessica? Would you be as cool with it as you are going to expect him to be?

"Fuck," I moaned out as Mike slid at least eight inches inside of me. "You feel so good, baby." I said as I put my arms around him.

"Remember, if you don't want to get caught," Mike whispered, "you have to keep it down."

"I know," I gasped as I did my best to contain the moans that desperately wanted to escape with each stroke.

I swear Mike fucked me in that bathroom in every way possible. After the first time I came, it's like the rational side of brain turned off so I could enjoy all the ways he kept twisting up my body while he made me cum more times than I could count.

One thing was for sure, Mike is definitely a very passionate and selfless lover.

I can't wait to see how he is when we don't have to sneak around or worry about getting caught.

Uh-oh.

See, Bitch. This is exactly what I was afraid of. You're already making plans for the next time, and you haven't even addressed the dozens of phone calls you've been avoiding from your husband?

Is Mike only doing this for the sex? Does he enjoy the fact that this relationship doesn't come with much since I am a married woman?

Did this nigga just snatch my soul out of my body and that is all I'm going to get out of this?

What normally happens after this?

What the fuck am I going to do now?

7

YOU CAN RUN, BUT YOU CAN'T HIDE

Mike and I used the hotel he got us for the night to fuck in every possible position. We did it on the balcony while we watched the sun rise. I almost broke my neck trying to keep my balance in the shower, and we finally decided to take a break after one of the hotel employees had addressed a noise complaint that came in from one of the rooms around us.

Are you going to ask him what to expect next after this, or do you plan on just going with the flow forever?

How do people typically handle this situation? I honestly never asked this man about his relationship status. Now, I want to know everything because this cannot be a one-time thing.

I wanted to ask him one of the millions of thoughts that were running through my mind, but I couldn't. My phone's incessant buzzing was proof my time in paradise had finally come to an end.

"Are you going to answer that," Mike asked as he put on his dress pants. "I'm sure your husband is probably worried."

He obviously has something he want to discuss also. God, I wish he would start it off so I wouldn't feel so awkward right now.

Almost all the calls have been from Donnell, and I'm sure he's fucking pissed off.

I won't ruin the rest of this time with Mike or stress myself about this afternoon's interview. I'll deal with it when I get back.

"I don't do this type of thing often, so there is a chance that he is upset or worried right now. I just have a lot going on today, and I don't want to kill this vibe," I responded.

"Should I assume that you'll also be avoiding this conversation with me about what's next with us," Mike asked as he zipped up his duffle bag. "I would hate for you to feel like I'm not trying to support you right now, but you're a very complex woman."

Great. He brought up my marriage again, but not exactly how I hoped he would have. This would have been so much easier if he would have started this off with what he wanted to happen next.

What the heck am I supposed to say? How is a married woman allowed to answer that question?

I've been dodging Donnell, and I know this conversation can't be any easier to have after I stayed out -again.

What do I do?

***

"Mrs. Bryant, thank you so much for meeting with me today," Chanel Weston, a local celebrity podcaster stated as the rest of her crew set up the lights for our interview.

Respectfully, I should have responded back with something like, "thank you so much for having me," but I just couldn't muster up the lie. Between the heat of the lights beaming down on us and the death glares coming from Donnell and Mike as they watched on, I was beginning to feel sick to my stomach.

To add to the already awkward situation, Jessica apparently had to be here for this.

Is he my husband or hers?

It's like I can never see Donnell without her tagging along somewhere close behind him. Do they want people to know what's going on?

Wait.

I guess that isn't fair when my ass hasn't returned a single one of that man's phone calls.

I was halfway down the rabbit hole of crazy thoughts when I saw it.

Mike and Donnell locked eyes. Then, Donnell glanced at me before looking back at Mike.

He knows it's him. He must know.

Anyway, doesn't Mike have anything else he could be doing right now? Does he enjoy watching me squirm or something? Why else would he be here?

Girl, slow your thoughts down because you're starting to sweat and you're clearly tripping. Mike is the reason behind a lot of these interviews that I've had lately. In fact, he's been to every single one that I've had. Donnell is usually working and misses these things.

As if Jessica had heard the crazy thoughts running through my mind, she gently caressed my back before whispering in my ear.

Was I that wrapped up in my thoughts that I didn't even notice when she walked my way?

Can I speak with you for a minute," Jessica asked without once pulling herself away.

Girl, can't you see that I'm doing the best that I can to avoid you, Donnell, and any conversation that we are supposed to have?

I wanted to run, but I knew I was trapped. I knew there was no way to leave this place without finally confronting some truths I had been running from.

"Can't you see that I'm getting ready for an interview," I responded as I moved away from her. "We should be starting any minute now, so it's not a good time," I declared.

Ok, bitch! I see you putting your foot down.

Before I had a moment to truly celebrate my small win, Chanel's nosey ass corrected me.

"Actually, we have about ten minutes before we start. It looks like my director is running a little last," she said as she checked her watch.

Oh, lucky me.

"Perfect," Jessica exclaimed as she grabbed my arm and led me to the back room. "I'll be quick."

***

Despite my initial reservations about the one-on-one talk before my interview, Jessica ended up saving me from sitting awkwardly in a room with Mike and Donnell. Anything was better than that, right?

"Girl," Jessica exclaimed as she closed the door and turned to look back at me. "What the hell is going on?"

Well, that relief didn't last long.

And anyway, bitch don't act concerned now. From where I'm sitting, you seem to be living your best life now that you can have all of Donnell's free time.

I desperately wanted to go off on her for her fake ass concern, but every time I got ready to open my mouth to speak, I just envisioned those cold, steel, cuffs on my wrist again.

"Didn't you say you wanted to talk to me," I asked while doing my best to mask my annoyance. "What do you need, Jessica? I'm trying to mentally prepare for this interview, so I'm not trying to talk about anything heavy or drama filled," I stated without looking her way.

Although I wasn't looking at her, I could feel her gaze piercing through me as I did my best to look busy checking my make-up.

"Your psychiatrist might enjoy this act that you're putting on," Jessica snapped back, "But I'm not a fan."

What the fuck did this bitch just say? Has Donnell been telling her about our therapy sessions?

"Excuse you," I asked as I put down my compact mirror and locked eyes with Jessica since the first time I arrived at the venue.

"You heard what the fuck I said," Jessica retorted without flinching or breaking eye contact. "Because you have to be one crazy motherfucker to invite me into your relationship only for you to jump ship and have a fucking attitude about it. What's going on, Katrina?

I thought you and I hit it off? Did I misread something," She asked as her tone and body language softened.

Oh shit! I've been thinking this is all about Donnell. Does Jessica really want something from me too?

"Jessica, were you expecting something from me relationally," I asked. "I just always assumed you were doing all of this to make Donnell happy. I just…" Before I could finish my sentence, Jessica stepped forward and planted the sweetest kiss on my lips.

"I've been lying to Donnell about your whereabouts to just keep things peaceful and easy for you, but I can't keep being your alibi if you won't even talk to me."

Wait. This woman has been lying to a man I know she loves and wants to be with to protect the relationship I have with him?

I'm confused as shit. I thought she wanted to be with him. I guess I didn't realize she wanted something from me too.

"Wait. Jessica," I started as I took a step back. "I'm seriously baffled by all of this. I thought you wanted Donnell, so I figured you were trying to hype up this threesome since that is what he wanted."

Jessica giggled. "You are clearly confused," she said before she extended her hand to ask for my mirror. "I'm solo poly, so while I do care for and want Donnell, I'm not that pressed for a partner that I need to chase pussy to get a nigga." Jessica paused for a moment to check her lipstick. "I'm doing all of this because I genuinely like you, Katrina. I just assumed the feeling was mutual since you were the one to reach out to me initially.”

For the first time since I met her, I looked Jessica up and down and I reminded myself of why I used to call her The Succubus. No one could deny how bad she is.

“Look, I’m just new to this whole thing. This world…or lifestyle of being poly just seems like a lot,” I responded as I took a seat on the plush couch in the venue’s private viewing room. “I don’t understand the rules or how to play, I guess.”

Jessica walked over and joined me on the couch. “The only reason this seems challenging is because you are avoiding the inevitable. If you plan on maintaining more than one relationship, that means you have to get comfortable with being vulnerable and having those uncomfortable conversations. Two things that are obviously a struggle for you.”

We both giggled at her last comment before a light knock on the other side of the door interrupted us.

“Two minutes until show time, Mrs. Bryant,” a voice on the other side stated firmly.

“Damn that was fast,” I declared as the butterflies in my tummy returned.

“See how fun communicating can be,” Jessica asked with a smile.

I gathered my things to head back to set.

“Listen, before you go,” Jessica started before I left the room. “Being a boss isn’t just about how well you fit in a dress or how mean your walk is. You have to start talking like one too. You’re in control here, baby. Start acting like it.”

***

“And there you have it folks,” Chanel Weston stated cheerfully. “Make sure you check out Katrina Bryant so you can find out for yourself why everyone who is somebody is fighting to book a spot on her calendar. Make sure you get in while you can or get mad when you have to Charge it to the Game!”

The lights above were too bright, so I never got to see the face behind the director’s station. I just heard him loudly yell out, “And cut,” before the set became chaotic as hell.

Before I knew it, almost every person in the live studio audience was headed straight to me to ask their questions and book a consultation.

As much as I wanted to revel in the moment of completing my

first celebrity interview, life was coming for me – fast.

"Great job sweetheart," Mike stated cheerfully as he softly grabbed my arm.

The look on his face said that he wanted to show his support with much more affection, but Donnell's gaze was locked in our direction.

I'm not sure what it was, but at that moment I wanted Mike to grab me like he had hours ago. The flashback of having his hands gripping my ass while he slammed me up and down on his dick made me horny all over again.

Stop trying to use Mike as a distraction. You have too much going on right now.

The look on Donnell's face is so hard to read. Is he angry about Mike being here? Is he excited to see me glowing up, or is he just trying to get Jessica and me naked and alone?

To my surprise, I spent almost two hours greeting potential clients. Who knew that people would listen to me, my story, and my struggles and care as much as they did?

When I started my business, it was all under the direction of Donnell. He saw the potential that was there and immediately went into overdrive to get my business set up for the big league and heavy hitting clients that he knew would be coming my way.

All of the excitement from birthing something new helped us take our relationship back to a place we only experienced in college. It took us back to a time when we were two crazy kids that were determined to take over the world together. We spent that weekend dreaming, creating, and making each other cum. For the first time in a long time, I felt like a priority to him. I was seen, heard, and understood by the only man I had ever planned a future with.

That one weekend had restored the hope that I had for Donnell and me. Well, that was until The Succubus called and he suddenly felt the need to make himself available to whatever she needed from him. Before I knew it, Jessica put my husband back under her spell, and the hope I had vanished right before my eyes.

I realize that I was originally down for this whole 'poly' thing, but that was before my husband love bombed me only to leave me hanging for the woman he's had by his side our entire marriage.

It was one thing when I speculated that my husband's late nights at the office were just an excuse to hide his affairs. Now that I know Donnell is with *her* when he's not with me or at home, just became too much. I'm already an overthinker, so this whole thing takes my brain into overdrive.

I was doing a great job of keeping it all together, but the more I thought about Donnell and the current state of our marriage, the more I wanted to run out of there and hide.

Look at them. If I wouldn't have known any better, I would have assumed that Jessica was Donnell's wife and not me.

Is this the life he's always envisioned with her? Was I just convenient until now?

Was that weekend with him real or was it all done to get us where we are today? Was it always their plot to slowly incorporate me into the life they were already living together?

The lump growing in my throat was becoming too hard to ignore anymore.

If I run out of here, Donnell and Mike are definitely going to follow.

If I start boo hoo crying, I'm going to look mentally unstable or something.

Fuck!

Running out of time, patience, and options, I did my best to casually excuse myself from the crowd.

"I'm going to step outside for some fresh air," I whispered to Mike. Just like the supportive man he was, he smiled back at me before he continued talking to the young black CEO that had just inquired about me designing her next home.

I glanced over to see Donnell and Jessica enjoying a conversation with the host, and I knew it was my only chance for a clean break.

With each determined step I took, I could hear Jessica's voice taunting me for running – yet again.

"Being a boss isn't just about how well you fill out your dress and how mean your walk is," her voice echoed in my head.

Well, maybe I'm not a boss after all then!

Wait. Am I talking back to this bitch's voice – in my head?

Have I officially lost my damn mind?

The moment I stepped outside and inhaled some fresh air, I immediately felt a sense of relief.

But I thought I wanted this?

Wasn't I the one who suggested she spend more time with him?

Regardless of how we got here, I had been an active participant with this process, so what is the problem now, Kat?

"The only reason this seems challenging is because you are

avoiding the inevitable," Jessica's advice started ringing in my ears again.

You're in control, baby.
Start acting like it.

8

TIL DEATH DO WE PART?

Hopefully ya'll know me enough to know that my crazy ass let all of Jessica's advice go in one ear and out of the other After all, I have too much shit going on right now that I can't allow myself to spend any more time in my feelings.

Thanks to almost six weeks of using my thriving business as an excuse, things are even crazier than ever. Donnell and I haven't really talked since before I went out of town with Mike, and can I keep it real? This break from him feels like the vacation that I've been waiting for. That's a bad thing, right?

If you answered yes, you aren't alone. Remember our therapist, Gabriella? Well, she agrees with you.

"Katrina, feeling a little anxiety when you have a difficult conversation with your spouse is normal. However, checking out of your marriage and still not having any desire to talk to your husband is not. What's *really* going on," Gabriella asked me during our weekly session. "You prioritize our meetings and your time with Mike and Jessica; however, you become so uneasy at the thought of talking to Donnell. Why do you think that is?"

Maybe because he won't fucking listen anyway.

Maybe it's because I don't know how to tell him that I don't think I want to do this anymore.

Maybe it's because I'm afraid that I'm wrong about Mike like I was about Donnell. Keeping things this way means that I never have to fail in either of those relationships.

Maybe I'm afraid to be alone.

I don't know! I thought it was her job to tell me what the problem was and then tell me how to fix it.

Kat, just shut the fuck up. It won't make sense to say it outloud anyway.

"Oh, I don't know," was all I could get out before Gabriella interjected.

"Katrina, I'm going to get paid regardless. As long as you are a respectful client, I will be here for you through your process. It benefits you nothing by lying to me and keeping all of those thoughts to yourself.

Contrary to popular beliefs, I'm not here to only listen. I'm also not here to tell you what to do."

Damn.

So then why the fuck do I come here every week?

"I'm here to be a safe space where you can sort out those thoughts," Gabriella continued. "I ask thought provoking questions, so I can help you think outside of the box. When you wrestle with them by yourself, you're just wasting your time and your money. Aren't you tired of doing that?"

"Tired of doing what exactly," I asked. I wanted to get clarity before I allowed myself to feel offended by her comments.

"Aren't you tired of wasting your life away? I mean, you gave your party years to Donnell because you only aspired to be a trophy wife. And can we be honest, most women who only aspire to be their husbands prize possession don't complain as much as you do. Those women usually let their husbands cheat in peace."

Is this bitch serious?

Am I paying this motherfucker to talk shit about me?

I sat there, stunned as Gabriella continued with her bullshit. I thought she was supposed to be a safe space? Why does it seem like she's judging me now?

"One minute, you say Donnell isn't even your type and he's not that great in bed. The next minute you want to be jealous of him screwing someone else," Gabriella said with a snicker.

If she says one more fucking thing, I'm going to give this bitch the fight she's obviously looking for.

"Oh, I don't even know why I waste my time with this," Gabriella said as she closed her notebook. "Your scary ass is just going to go home, overthink this entire situation, and show up next week for me to do it all over again. You love tormenting yourself like this because you don't believe you deserve any better. That's why you settle for mediocre dick, a mediocre marriage, and now mediocre side lovers."

Katrina, we don't look good in orange, and we hate the feeling of those cold cuffs on our wrist.

Just shut the fuck up.

"From where I'm sitting, Mike sounds like the kind of man that women dream about. But you are too busy convincing yourself that you don't deserve the love that he's giving you. That's why you are telling yourself that he's only a distraction. That way you don't feel bad about sabotaging something you claim to want. If you don't know what to do with him," is all I let her say before I finally spoke up.

"Bitch! You have a lot of fucking nerve to sit up there talking shit about me when I'm dropping a bill to sit in these dusty ass chairs that should have been replaced three seasons ago.

Matter of fact, your whole office is tacky as hell. You wouldn't know good taste if it slapped you in the face. And it's so cute how you have so much to say about my nigga problems. Bitch, do you even have one? Since we are now in the business of judging each other, I can tell you with confidence that you can't have a nigga worth bragging about because nothing in this entire space is worth half of what I have on right now."

I wanted to keep going, but I could feel something brewing inside of me that I was not used to feeling.

"Ha," Gabriella chuckled. "You want to brag about money? You deserve at least that after giving away your good years to a man who puts up more of a fight for his side bitches then he does his wife."

"How dare you," I roared back in anger. "I didn't just give him my *good years*. I loved him despite his imperfections because he loved me back. Donnell didn't leave every time we had a problem, and he made sure that I always had what I wanted."

I had more to say, but I chose to stop instead. The anger that was beginning to absorb every part of my body was becoming too much for me to handle. I wasn't sure if I wanted to punch her, scream, or murder her with the words I was holding back. Because I rarely allowed myself to feel angry, I wasn't sure what I was capable of in that moment.

"Katrina," Gabriella said as she adjusted herself in her seat. "Do you realize that the love you described is exactly what he gives to Jessica? He's always been there, and he provides for her also. Truthfully, if it was only about those two things you should be completely satisfied with Mike, but here you are."

I can't tell if this is a part of her therapist shit or not, but I need her to tread lightly with me. With the way I'm feeling right now, she is liable to get slapped, and I will smile in my mug shot.

"Watch your mouth, Gabriella," I shot back. "If you keep playing with me, you're going to meet a side of me that you won't like."

"Katrina, please. You don't believe that yourself. We all know that the thought of going back to jail is enough to shut you down. That's why you let people walk all over you.

Don't try to act big with me now, you need to save this energy with me and direct it to your husband. Or is he Jessica's now? I'm confused," Gabriella shot back.

"You are a lot more than just confused if you think that I'm just going to continue to allow this," I declared. "I pay enough money to your company to get some fucking respect while I'm here."

"Katrina," Gabriella started again. "It doesn't matter how much money you have. You can't buy anyone's respect. Why don't you feel like your worthy of it just because of who you are? Why do you have to attach it to a price tag?"

She's definitely doing her therapist shit, but she's pushed me too far to the edge. She's going to deal with the mess she created – today.

"Who the fuck said that I was attaching respect to a price tag," I asked. "I just needed you to remember who the fuck I am and how I've been helping you pay your bills!"

"As cute as your monologue sounds," Gabriella started, "It's Donnell's name on the checks that you've been writing me. So, you might as well add me to the list of names of women he takes care of, I guess.

Does that make me one of your sister wives now or have you guys still not talked that through yet?"

That's it!

"I will never have a sister wife," I declared as I stood to my feet. "The best thing that I've ever done was allow Donnell this freedom. It birthed in me the things I needed to change my life. I don't have to sit around waiting for his ass to give me breadcrumbs whenever he feels like it. Bitch, I make my own money and my own rules now. If I want a mediocre marriage with a fine ass nigga on the side, that's what I'm going to do."

Ya'll don't judge that last comment, please. This is new territory for me, remember? Obviously, that's not the kind of marriage I want to have, but I'm so fucking tired of losing. I refuse to be defeated by Gabriella right now.

"I no longer need to choose men because of their social status or tax bracket," I continued. "I'm enough on my own, so I don't have to sit around waiting for any man. I'm the fucking boss now. Get it?" And yes, ya'll I said it with as much confidence as you just read it in.

Gabriella stood up to her feet as she began clapping. "Good job Katrina, I know you feel good getting that out!"

She was right, but the anger I was still feeling in that moment wouldn't allow me the chance to tell her that.

"It's Ok," Gabriella stated as she sat down and pulled out her notebook. "You have a lot of emotions running through you right now, so I'm not taking any of this personally.

Conversations are not scary. Asking for what you deserve it not scary. For a long time, you've chosen to fight with those thoughts on your own instead of using your voice to speak up for yourself. Do you notice how your mind probably isn't racing with a million questions right now?"

She was right. The usual chatter box in my brain had finally shut up for a moment.

"It's so much easier to be present when you can decipher between your own voice and the anxiety that *will* drive you crazy if you allow it to run freely," Gabriella said before she feverishly jotted down her notes.

I took a deep sigh of relief. Regardless of how I got here, I felt good.

"Now that you realize you are a boss who is worthy of the love she gives other people, what are you going to do now, boss lady?"

***

As if the universe had sent out a cosmic message that I was in a great headspace, Donnell and Jessica were quick to kill that moment. Before I could make it to my car, I had already missed two calls from Jessica.

Katrina, you are worthy of peace and love, and you have the right to remove yourself from spaces that don't provide that to you.

I took another deep breath before I called her back.

"Girl, where are you at," Jessica yelled into the phone. "You are not going to believe this shit."

I really can't enjoy peace for more than a minute, huh?

"I'm on my way to my office," I said as I jumped into my brand-new G-Wagon.

"Well, I'm in front of your office right now. You're not gonna believe this, but Donnell is cheating on us!"

***

I was completely unbothered by the bomb Jessica dropped on me. Maybe it was the freedom I felt after therapy, or maybe it was because this is something I've always had to deal with. Either way, I now knew that this no longer had to be my reality if I didn't want to participate anymore.

In the last few weeks, I have been busy making all kinds of upgrades. My huge office in the center of downtown Orlando was one of them.

I was halfway to my suite when I heard Jessica crying in the hallway.

Try to have some patience with her, Katrina. While we are used to Donnell doing this, she clearly has no idea who he truly is.

"Why didn't you ask my assistant to let you in," I asked as I pulled her in for a hug. "You didn't have to stand out here like this."

She didn't immediately respond. Instead, she sunk into my embrace and cried for a moment.

"Let's take this into the office, so you can tell me everything," I said as I grabbed her hand and walked into the suite.

"Good afternoon Mrs. Bryant. You're three o'clock appointment is running a little late," my assistant, Alyssa started as soon as I walked in the door.

"Can you hold everything for the next hour," I asked as I rushed by her desk. "I have a lot going on."

Before she could rebuttal, I pulled Jessica into my office to finish the conversation.

"Ok," I said as I put my stuff down and sat in my large leather seat. "Tell me exactly what happened."

"Well," Jessica began as she tried to hold back her tears. "Last night, Donnell told me that we couldn't spend any time together because he was going to spend the night with you. Obviously, I didn't question anything because I was glad that you had finally decided to speak to him again. It wasn't until you text me this morning that I knew there was no way he was ever with you. When I confronted him about it, he shrugged it off. I guess he figures that because I'm poly it's not a big deal."

"I'm not going to lie sis," I started. "I'm kind of confused myself. If you are in relationships with multiple people, why do you care if he is seeing someone else?"

Jessica chuckled between her sobs. "Just because I am in relationships with multiple people doesn't give one of my partners a right to lie to me. Every successful relationship is built on certain foundations. Trust is a part of that. How can I trust someone if I can't believe the things that they tell me?

Hell, if anything that makes me even more mad about the situation. I see other people, so he has no reason to lie!"

As much as I wanted to sympathize with Jessica, I just couldn't relate to her. At the end of my therapy session, I felt a sense of peace wash over me when all my usual thoughts vanished and the only one that remained said, *I want a divorce.*

When that thought crossed my mind, I didn't make that decision because of what I feel for Mike. I didn't allow Jessica or her needs to be a part of that decision. I made it on my own because I know it's the best thing for me.

As I'm building this beautiful empire from the ground up, I see how powerful I am. In fact, sitting in this chair, watching this woman break down over Donnell was a reminder that I never wanted him or anyone else to have that much dominance over me ever again.

"Why don't you seem bothered by this," Jessica asked as she wiped away more tears from her eyes.

Because this nigga has been cheating on me since I met him. Like he's already admitted to me before, he likes to enjoy a taste of something new when he can. This is never going to change about him.

I wanted to tell her the truth. I wanted to let her know that when we decided to bring her into this, we never discussed an ongoing relationship. He only ever wanted sex out of this, and I saw a way that I could explore my fantasies while he was occupied. I didn't plan to form this intimate friendship with her; it just happened.

"I dunno," I lied as I grabbed my phone to avoid making eye contact with her. "I guess I'm just too busy to care right now."

"Bullshit," Jessica replied. "I know Mike has been spoiling the shit out of you, but we've had enough conversations that I know you care for Donnell. What's up?"

Before I could answer her question, Alyssa paged me.

"Mrs. Bryant, I have a delivery of twelve dozen roses, where should I put all of these flowers?"

I wanted to hide the smile the crept on my face, but I just couldn't. Mike faithfully sent me flowers weekly, and with the last delivery still on display throughout the office, I wasn't sure where I would be able to put all of them.

This moment felt like the confirmation that I need. For years, I had allowed Donnell to stress me out to the point that my weight would fluctuate or cause my edges to thin. Now, I have a man who goes out of his way to make my day – every day. It doesn't matter if we've had a disagreement, or if there is a new attractive assistant in his office. He tells me and he shows me that I am what he wants.

I deserve to feel loved, appreciated, seen, and valued. I deserve this love that Mike gives me, and I'm going to appreciate it for as long as I have it because I've waited long enough to experience it.

I deserve this.

"Well, I guess that smile on your face is everything I needed to know," Jessica stated before she cleared her throat.

Before I could respond, Alyssa came through my desk phone's intercom again.

"Sorry to keep bugging you Mrs. Bryant. You just received a single white Orchid. Should I put this anywhere special?"

I haven't talked to Donnell in weeks. Now that his side piece caught him slipping, he wants to send me flowers?

I did my best to hide the annoyance on my face, but Jessica immediately knew what was going on.

"Those are from Donnell, huh," she asked.

I can't lie. I have to tell her the truth.

"Alyssa, can you please bring that last delivery to my desk," I asked before releasing the page button.

"I don't want to assume, but I'm pretty sure they are," I responded as I sat back in my chair and waited to see what lie Donnell put on the card this time.

"If you were me," Jessica started as she adjusted herself in her seat, "What would you do?"

I would consider it a fucking blessing that you have a clear break from this man, his lies, and his selfishness.

Like the lifesaver that she is, Alyssa interrupted the conversation again by placing the flowers on my desk.

Jessica couldn't hide her anxiousness if she tried. She looked like she wanted to jump over my desk to read the card for herself.

Damn.

I remember acting just like this not too long ago. How the hell does Donnell get beautiful women to just give up their self-esteem and self-worth for him?

If I had any doubt that the flowers were from Donnell, the cheap looking Orchid was just the confirmation that I needed.

I grabbed the card and opened the envelope.

"Well, what does it say," Jessica asked in anticipation.

"Sorry, but you know how I can be," I said as I read the card out loud.

You have got to be fucking kidding me? You mean to tell me this man won't even pretend to act romantic? He obviously believes that I will be ok with this behavior, and I refuse to allow him to think that anymore.

***

"I want a divorce," I declared while Donnell ate his dinner. Sitting across from him in the house that I once prayed for felt so different this time around. For one, it had been weeks since I had laid eyes on him. It looked like he was beginning to put on some weight around his midsection, and it looked like he hadn't been to the barbers either. He looked a mess.

To my surprise, my shocking statement didn't bother him. In fact, he just kept eating as if I hadn't said a thing.

Ok, Katrina! I see you using your words like the boss bitch that you are! You better let people know how you feel and stand on it!

"How has business been for you," Donnell asked before he scooped another bite of rice and chicken into his already stuffed mouth.

What did I ever see in him?

"Business has been great, and that's exactly why I think this is the best time to agree to put this chapter of our lives behind us," I responded.

"That's good," he responded flatly. "I'm going to need some work done at my office next week. Tomorrow I'll reach out and have Alyssa add it to your calendar."

I know this motherfucker heard me. Why is he ignoring me?

"Did you hear what I said about wanting a divorce," I asked him clearly.

"I heard you, but I'm going to finish eating and then I'm going to get my dick wet by you. I'll decide when it's time for us to get a divorce." Without missing a beat, he continued to eat his food.

Let me get this straight. This bitch just got caught with another whore and he thinks I'm giving him pussy tonight?

How have I allowed him to think this is ok?

What am I supposed to do now? I spoke up. I made my wants clear, and he is just choosing not to accept it.

I could feel the anger brewing inside of me again. It seemed to get stronger with each bite that he took.

"Well, I suggest you call whatever whore Jessica caught you with. I have no desire to fuck you ever again." I declared as I pushed my plate from in front of me. I could no longer hide the disgust that I was feeling.

"Katrina, who the fuck are you talking to," Donnell asked as he grabbed his napkin to clean his mouth. "I haven't complained about my wife running around like a cheap whore, so you won't complain about what I do. I pay every damn bill in this house. You're going to give me pussy when I want, and without issue. Got it?"

This is exactly how I've stayed trapped in this situation with his ass. Any other time, I didn't have the money or resources to go anywhere else. That's why he's been allowed to talk to me however he wants to.

Not anymore.

"No." I responded back confidently. "In fact, I'm going to excuse myself, so I can pack a bag for the night. This conversation is obviously pointless."

I didn't wait for him to respond. I stood up, grabbed my plate, and made my way to the kitchen. I was halfway to the sink when I heard dishes breaking on our marble floors.

"This is what's wrong with you bitches," I heard Donnell scream out from the other room. "You get a little money, and you let it go to your head."

Did he just call me a bitch? He's never done that before.

And what the fuck am I supposed to do now? I've struggled with speaking up for myself for years. Gabriella didn't tell me what to do when someone responds to my truth this way.

"Just clean this shit up and be ready to suck my dick in an hour," Donnell continued.

Oh, hell no! You can't let it end like this because he'll think he can do this again. He also won't take me serious about wanting a divorce. Speak up now, Kat. Or be prepared to be one of his little bitches forever.

I wanted to scream, shout, and call him everything but a child of God. The anger I was feeling inside should have allowed me to, but I just couldn't. Instead, I had to fight just to muster up the courage to tell him no.

"No," Donnell, I said from the kitchen. "Again, I'm going to excuse myself, and pack a bag for the night." My voice didn't show it, but I was terrified.

Now what?

The house went silent. I imagined that Donnell was thinking of his next move, but he is usually quick on his feet.

Just continue doing what you're doing, Kat.

Breathe in.

Breathe ok.

You're ok.

I took a few deep breaths before deciding to go pack my bag. I was almost out of the kitchen when he met me face-to-face at the doorway.

"You must have lost your fucking mind," Donnell growled as his presence suddenly felt like something I should fear.

Breath in and out, Kat. No matter what, you have to stand up for yourself.

In all the time that we have been together, Donnell has never approached me in this way. The anger in his eyes and the tone of his voice was not something I had ever experienced with him.

Has he always been like this, and I never noticed because I was too busy playing the role he expected me to play forever? Is this how he treats me when I decide to put myself first?

I'm not going to lie, staring down an angry stranger was terrifying. But ya'll know what scares me more than not knowing his next move? I would hate to imagine a life where he believes that he can bully me into submission.

I opened my mouth to say something, but before I could Donnell responded.

"Kat, just shut the fuck up," Donnell spat before I could say anything. In fact, because he was so close to my face, I felt the droplets of his saliva with each syllable.

Kat, just shut the fuck up.

In that moment, all I could do was think about each time I had said that to myself. *Kat, just shut the fuck up.* That's when it hit me. That thought wasn't my own. Donnell has been responding to me like this for as long as I've known him. Hell, he's said it so much that I usually say it to myself now. *Kat, just shut the fuck up.*

It's no wonder I never stood up for myself, he's gotten so deep into my head that I regurgitate the shit for him. *Kat, just shut the fuck up.*

I could suddenly feel the anger inside of me beginning to boil over.

I've allowed this puny bastard to believe that he has this much authority over me. This nigga really thinks I'm supposed to shut up just because he said so? Guess what? Katrina is tired of shutting the fuck up. You're going to hear what I have to say whether you like it or not.

"Counselor," I started as I hoped to speak to Donnell's common sense. "Let me remind you that here in the state of Florida, you could be prosecuted for that saliva you just left on my face.

I could see it now," I continued while I took a few steps back from Donnell. "Attorney Attacks Wife and is Charged with Battery, or they could make me the star and say something like Celebrity Stylist Attacked by Jealous Husband After Asking for Divorce. Which headline do you think they'll go with?"

***

"Katrina, you did what," Gabriella asked through tears while she tried her hardest to stop laughing.

"I told that son of a bitch that if he didn't back the fuck up I was not only going to divorce him, but I was also going to make a fucking show of it. I told him I would ask for my half of his firm and the house before exposing how ugly he can really be," I stated with confidence.

It had been three months since Donnell and I had the show down in our kitchen that day, and a lot has happened. For one, I don't even have time for therapy every week anymore. Before you say anything crazy, I'm trying to make more time. I've just been busy traveling the world, staying booked with clients, and closing this chapter of my life for good.

Last month, we closed on the sale of our home, and while it was bittersweet, I used my half of the proceeds to make a down payment on a condo in New York! Although I've never shared my dreams with others, I've always wanted a high rise in the city. Now, I have my own. I don't have slave to serve a man a hot meal to have what I want because it's in my name. That's right, baby. These days I only suck dick because I want to!

It's crazy how much a person can grow when they are placed in the right environment. Now that I don't have to constantly worry about Donnell and his forever changing needs, I don't feel like I'm constantly at war with my own thoughts. Shit, now that I don't have him feeding me bullshit, I can recognize which ones are actually mine.

I bet you want to know about Jessica, huh? Well, I wish I had more to tell you about that situation. After I formally filed for divorce, I received a text message from her that said she was no longer "allowed" to speak to me. Apparently, Donnell gave her an ultimatum. She had to choose and judging from the lack of activity on her social media accounts, it looks like she chose to jump into my old role.

I think the hardest part of this divorce has been losing her friendship and everything that I thought she was. It's crazy to think that the vixen I knew and admired doesn't exist anymore. A week after that text, she deleted all her sexy pictures off Instagram, and she removed anything having to do with her business. She was no longer the ultra-confident, boss that I had met or been attracted to. Now, she's just doing whatever she has to in order to keep Donnell happy. Sad, isn't it?

For now, I plan to keep seeing Mike. I love the way he shows his affection and gratitude for our connection. Shit, now that I don't have Donnell in the picture, Mike has been booking hotels, following me all over the world and breaking my back on every single balcony.

Don't get it twisted, I like Mike, but we are not in a relationship. I have to stress that because after I filed for divorce every eligible bachelor that was worth at least seven figures reached out to personally offer their "condolences" about my marriage ending. While I do enjoy the stability that he offers, I did just get out of a marriage. Telling a man like Mike that I wasn't ready for a committed relationship was hard because I know men like him are not easy to find. But this woman I am becoming daily means more to me than any man ever could.

Although I never got to explore Jessica in the way that I had fantasized, our time together changed me in a way that I didn't know was possible. Do you remember that little homework assignment Jessica had me try? You know, the one where I had to find the porno I liked and explore myself sexually? Yeah, well it turns out that it comes in handy because I'm a morning person. And I like it every morning. That's why whether I wake up with a nigga in my bed or not, I always start the day by softly caressing my thighs before I make my way up to my breasts. I'll slowly roll on to my back in anticipation for the energy I'll have after I cum. As always, *she'll* be warm, wet, and eager for my touch. I'll play with myself while I listen to what my body needs that day. Sometimes I like it fast and rough. Some mornings I just take my time. Either way, I'll give my body exactly what it desires. Then, when I know I'm about to explode, I'll use my other hand to grab my ass. I'll let out a little moan because something about hearing, "umm-hmm" when I'm about to nut takes me over the edge. While I'm creaming on myself, I always take the time to remind myself, "Nobody fucks this pussy as good as I fuck this pussy." It's my own declaration and reminder that I am mine before I am anyone else's. In a time where powerful women like Jessica are willing to exchange their marital status for someone to control their body, this is my act of defiance.

"So," Gabriella started as she broke me out of the trance I was in. "Your divorce is almost finalized. You purchased your own home, and just opened another office in Manhattan. Now what?

She forgot to mention my Forbes article, my product line in Macy's and my Oprah interview. But can you believe that I'm really out here doing the shit I wanted my partner to do? Bitch, I became the motherfucker I was attracted to!

"Good question," I said as I sat back in my chair. "I guess the best way to answer that is I'm just going to continue walking the walk and talking the talk of the true boss bitch I am."

Nympho

KEAIDY BENNETT

$\underline{1}$

OBSESSION VS ADDICTION

Olivia sat on the cold steel table, fighting back the hot tears that were waiting to explode. After all, to her, crying was a weak trait; and Olivia Perez was far from weak.

"I know this is difficult for you, but keep in mind that I was your friend before I became your doctor. We've been like sisters since we were five, and I've always stood by your side. Let me help you through this," Dr. Janet Brown said, taking a seat beside Olivia.

"This can't be real. This is just some kind of sick joke, right?" Olivia asked as she stared at her best friend, frozen in disbelief. "This kind of stuff happens to other people, but it's not supposed to happen to me."

"Come on Liv. You know I would never play about something as serious as this. I know how you are, but trust me, you need to talk to someone about this.

As your doctor, I'm telling you this is crucial and requires constant medical attention. Talking to someone else will make it a lot easier to work through your emotions. Not speaking to anyone is not going to make your problem go away.

And as your friend, I'm telling you that I already made you an appointment with this great counselor. She's cool, professional, very knowledgeable, and easy to talk to." Janet handed her a business card and held her friend's hand longer than she would have with anyone else.

Janet knew Olivia well enough to know that she was ready to cuss her out at the mere suggestion that she attend therapy. Still, she also knew how desperately her friend needed help.

***

"So, tell me why you're here," Daniella asked.

To Olivia's own surprise, she not only took the card from her friend without telling her where she thought it should go, but she took the advice to see a counselor. Luckily, Daniella seemed to be everything Janet had promised.

"I like having sex," Olivia stated bluntly. "A lot of sex."

"What do you consider to be a lot?" Daniella asked as she shifted slightly in her chair.

"I have sex at least four times a day. I'll do it anywhere with any good-looking and in-shape male that I encounter."

For years, Olivia had rationalized her high sex drive. Now, hearing it out loud as she confessed such a dark secret to a complete stranger caused her to finally face the horrible truth: she didn't just like sex; she was addicted to it.

"Is there any particular trait other than him being in-shape that you like in a sexual partner?"

Embarrassed by her answer, it took Olivia a few moments to make another terrible confession. "I just care if he has the endurance to match my stamina so that I can cum. I don't like a boring fuck, and I need as much ass slapping and grabbing as I do sensual kisses. I also love to feel his teeth firmly clasped around my skin."

Daniella watched as Olivia squirmed on the oversized leather couch with her eyes closed as if she weren't just telling a story but reliving it, too.

"I love fucking in public places because the mere thought of being caught is enough for me to get off.

The first thing I'll notice about the man is his scent. One whiff of some sexy cologne and it immediately makes me think of how victorious I'll feel once he's musky from all the sweat we'll produce from our adventurous sex.

The next thing I notice are his hands. I love large, strong, working-man hands caressing every part of my delicate skin. After that, I then look at his lips because I imagine feeling them on every square inch of me."

Olivia's arousal was obvious to Daniella by how many times she seemed to fight the urge to slide her hand all the way up her gray pencil skirt to the warm, now wet center of her that was just dying for attention.

Olivia opened her eyes and took a few moments to regain her composure. Once she snapped out of her trance, she felt like a freak-show as she assumed that Daniella was probably uncomfortable with all of the information she had just shared. Olivia began frantically tugging on her outfit as if she could hide in her clothes. Realizing that her small outfit choice wasn't going to provide the relief she was silently praying for, she reached for her purse.

"I don't need some uppity bitch judging me because I've mastered the art of how-to cum. I know how to do it by myself, and I know how to provide it to my partners. I'm so good at what I do that I become an addiction for these men because they know they'll never be able to meet a bitch who can put it down like me!"

Daniella got up from her chair and joined Olivia on the large leather couch. "Please don't leave," she pleaded as she gently placed a hand on her shoulder. "I'm not judging you. I genuinely just want to help you through this. Trust me. I've helped others through this same process before."

"You can't help me," Olivia snapped. "Because I don't need any fucking help. I love to fuck, and I'm good at it. If that makes me a whore in your book, then just make sure you know I'm the best whore you'll ever fucking meet!"

"You're not a whore, Olivia. You're a woman who loves sex more than most, and it doesn't make you a bad person at all. Just like any other addiction, it's only pollution in the brain. I can help you get over this. Please just let me help you."

Although Olivia loved sex, she had never been intimate with a woman before. It wasn't until Daniella was sitting so close to her did she have a chance to notice just how attractive she was.

Her beautiful, thick, caramel legs told Olivia that Daniella had to work out for her to have the legs of a goddess.

Her Dolce and Gabbana perfume danced around Olivia's nostrils. It instantly caused her to envision how something so sweet could ever smell musky at all. She imagined how many hours she would have to put in to find out if it were possible. Since she hadn't been to the gym yet, she knew she had the energy to do whatever she needed to find out.

The warmth of Daniella's body brought on a level of heat Olivia had never felt before. The only help she wanted from Daniella was to relieve herself of it by throwing her pretty ass across the large cherry desk in the room and pleasing her body. She wanted to do it so well that the only addiction that would need to be cured would be Daniella's addiction to the magic inside of Olivia's tongue.

Daniella firmly grasped Olivia's shoulder to break her out of the fantasy she was clearly stuck in. Unbeknownst to her, that touch by her soft, manicured hand was all it took to cause an inferno between Olivia's thighs.

"Get the fuck off of me!" Olivia screamed out. Since she lost her virginity at the tender age of fourteen, she had never ignored her body's urge for sex. It was taking everything in her to avoid her body's natural response to someone as attractive as Daniella.

Without giving her any more time to object her decision, Olivia darted out of the office to her car. She pulled out her phone and sent a text to her most reliable sex partner.

"Meet me at the gym NOW!"

***

"Olivia how long do you think I can keep doing this? You know I want more than this—," Kevin stated before Olivia cut him off.

"Shut the fuck up. Pull those pants off and fuck me damn it. I'm not here for all of that."

Olivia and Kevin had been fucking since they were teenagers. Because of that, there relationship was a little messier than Olivia was used to dealing with. For years, Kevin has been vocal about his desire for more than their closet affairs, but Olivia knew she could never give him what he wanted.

Even though she was beginning to accept that fact that she loved sex more than most people do, she had always known that she was not ok with a man being in control of when or with who she could catch a nut with.

"Who the fuck do you think you are barking out orders at me like I'm some fucking dog?" Kevin's voice boomed through the small, dark utility closet inside of the gym they both frequented. "You can throw around demands to those bitch-ass employees of yours, but you're in the presence of a king, and you will do whatever the fuck I tell you to. Do you got that?"

"Yes daddy," Olivia replied timidly.

That was what she loved most about him. He knew exactly how to put her in her fucking place. His 6'5 stature and large muscular frame meant that they never had sex in the same boring positions. Once he started demanding things from her, it meant he was getting ready to fuck her in every way imaginable in that tight space and Olivia was ready for it.

"You know I hate when you act like that. It almost makes me want to punish you." He stripped out of his sweatpants and white wife-beater.

Kevin had the darkest skin Olivia had ever seen. That delicious chocolate complexion covered every part of him, even down to his large member.

"Get on your knees and beg for it," he demanded.

"Please give it to me, daddy. I promise I'll never make that mistake again. Dámelo por favor papí," Olivia begged.

He grabbed the back of her head and tried to force all nine and a half inches inside of her mouth. She gagged once to give her throat more space to fill him up, and it only took a few seconds. Still, Olivia found her rhythm and began sucking and slurping on his dick like it was crucial for her survival.

"Damn, baby," Kevin whispered. "You know exactly how I like it. Get up so I can make love to you."

Olivia rolled her eyes and ignored his request because she had no desire to have anyone make love to her. She just wanted him to shut the fuck up so she could cum.

"Please let me make love to you right now, Liv," he softly pleaded again.

Olivia wasn't sure what aggravated her more. Maybe it was the fact that he was begging instead of giving her what she needed or that it was usually easier for her to not care about his desire for more of her.

She pulled his penis from the back of her throat, stood up, and slapped the shit out of him.

"Save the sensual shit for your other bitches. I just want you to fuck me, tell me what to do, and choke me. Why are you making this so fucking hard? Kevin, we've been doing this shit forever. Aren't you tried of doing this and ruining our moments together?"

Kevin took his right hand and clasped it firmly around her neck while pushing her back against the door.

Olivia grabbed onto his shoulders while he helped get her legs wrapped around his waist. That way he could enter her just like she wanted.

"Yes daddy," she moaned softly. His grip around her throat was firmer than usual, but to Olivia, pain meant pleasure, and she loved every minute of it.

"You're a selfish bitch," Kevin replied angrily. "You only care about yourself and getting off."

Normally, Olivia would have had a mouthful for the disrespect he just dished out at her; however, she was close to an orgasm and could care less about any words coming out of his mouth.

"Enjoy this nut bitch because it will be the last one you ever get from me. I'm fucking tired of sitting around waiting for you to tell me when I can have more of you." With each word that he spoke, it was as if he pounded with more passion and intensity. "I'm tired of just waiting by and watching other people experience you in the way that I want you."

Instead of holding her around her hips like he usually would have when they were in this position, Kevin never once removed his hand from around her neck. As his thrust got harder, his grip got tighter, and even through the poorly lit space, she could see the anger burning through his eyes.

"I want you and all of you, and you just want this dick. I know that I can give you the world if you'd let me. I'd fill you with love and shower you with gifts, but instead, I can only fill you with my meat and shower you in my cum.

You want to be fucked like some cheap slut? Then I'll give you exactly what you want, bitch."

At first, Olivia only cared about her orgasm. Now, she was trying to prevent herself from passing out due to the lack of oxygen. She began using the little strength she had remaining to slap his hands from her neck, but it was all in vain.

"Don't change your mind now. I'm giving you exactly what you asked for. You just wanted dick, right? Well, take all of this dick, you fucking slut."

Desperate for air, Olivia began knocking over the items on the shelf next to her so she could hopefully get someone to rescue her. As she felt herself about to slip into the darkness that was calling her, she got exactly what she had been praying for. Jeffery, one of the club's personal trainers, pushed his way through the door, causing them to both fall back on the cold floor.

Kevin was dressed and out of there before Olivia could actually make out what all was happening around her. Once she finally snapped back to reality, she heard Jeffery asking her a question with sincere concern.

"Yes," she shouted as she lowered her skirt that had been hiked above her waist. "Yes, I really do need help!"

***

Luckily for Olivia, Jeffery had been very understanding with her wish to not call the police. Instead, he sat down next to her and allowed Olivia to cry until she had emptied herself of all her sadness. He knew Olivia from training and fucking her a few times, and she had expressed how bad the incident could be for her business. She didn't even want to think of the clients she could have possibly lost over such a scandal. No one would care to hire a PR agent who couldn't manage her own image.

"I'm glad to see that you've changed your mind," Daniella said as Olivia walked through the door of her plush downtown office.

"You can save the smart remarks for your patients who are eager to go through this with you," Olivia retorted. "I just finally realized that I genuinely do need the help.

If you are serious about helping me, then you need to never look or smell as good as you do right now. I mean it," Olivia demanded as she sat down on the leather couch, making sure to leave on her sunglasses so Daniella couldn't see her puffy, swollen eyes.

After crying in the closet for at least twenty minutes, Olivia thought it was best to see Daniella right away. She didn't know how she would ever make it through the night without trying to have sex again if she didn't get someone else to intervene.

"Deal," Daniella said, agreeing to her terms. "I'm willing to do whatever it takes to make sure that you're successful on your road to recovery. Did anything happen that caused you to have such a change of heart?"

"Look, lady," Olivia said sharply as she began to lose her cool. More than anything, Olivia wanted desperately just wanted to forget the last two hours of her life. "I changed my mind, and I realized that I need help. Shouldn't that be the only important part of this entire conversation?"

"It absolutely is, but I also want to make sure that you know that I can't help you if you're not honest with me."

"I got it," Olivia responded. "Now that you've gotten that disclosure out of the way, can we move on, please?"

"Sure, but before we begin, I just want to tell you a few things. I'm not here to judge you. I only want to help you through this. Talk to me just like you would with one of your girlfriends, and then I won't have to seem so invasive by asking you a trillion questions. Everything we discuss is strictly confidential unless you become a danger to yourself or others."

"Yeah. Yeah. I got it," Olivia responded. Can we get on to the important stuff now?"

"Ok. I'm glad to see this change of energy," Daniella stated. " Why don't you start off by telling me exactly why you're here and searching for help today."

"But you know exactly why I'm here," Olivia snapped back. "I thought we discussed all of that earlier this morning?"

"Yes, but as cliché as it sounds, that verbal confirmation that you have a problem really is the first step in the right direction. I can sit here and ramble on forever about what textbooks say are the symptoms of sexual addiction, but it's not going to be the same as you can admitting that on your own."

Olivia was at a loss for words. Up until two hours ago, she sincerely didn't see any issues with her behavior. She really just enjoyed having sex and didn't think she should feel like a creep for being great at what she loved.

"I don't know." Olivia stated softly. "I don't think that I'm ready to do that yet."

"Then I can't help you," Daniella said bluntly as she closed her notebook. "Look, I'm leading a meeting tonight with other individuals who are in a similar situation as you. I challenge you this: if you can go the next four hours without a mere thought of sex, then I'll leave you alone. If you happen to find yourself fantasizing about it at all, then I expect to see you at the meeting tonight." Daniella handed Olivia a small plain card with the address and time of the meeting.

"Bet," Olivia said, accepting her challenge. It was only for four hours. How hard could it really be?

***

After leaving Daniella's office, Olivia decided that after all she endured that day, she needed some retail therapy.

"Good afternoon Ms. Perez," Nick, the boutique's owner, greeted her. "Is there anything in particular that I could help you with today or are you just exploring today?"

She knew just what he meant by his offer. After all, they had sex every time she came into his store.

Typically, knowing her ability to perform sexually gave her a massive boost to her ego. Now, for the first time ever, she was truly embarrassed by it.

"No, thank you," she said as she walked towards the back of the store to see his selection of evening gowns.

Surprised by her rejection of his usual advance, he moved from behind the counter, followed her, and gently pressed himself behind her.

"All of my employees are off today, and I'm getting ready to close for the day. We can turn off the lights and do it everywhere in here," Nick whispered softly in Olivia's ear as he ran his hands down the front of her skirt to the sweet spot he was aching for.

"I would love to, but I don't have that kind of time today," Olivia lied, hoping he would get the clue so she wouldn't have to reject any more of his advances.

"I'll be quick," he retorted before he began kissing Olivia's neck softly.

At that moment, all Olivia could think about was how the way his dick curved made it impossible for him to miss her spot. She slid her hand down his thigh until she felt what she was looking for.

"Hmm," Nick moaned into her ear. "Take these fucking clothes off."

Olivia loved how sex with Nick was amazing and without any emotional attachments. Nick was unhappily married, but every divorce lawyer in the state he spoke with gave him the same advice: "It's cheaper to keep her." Because of that, Nick never asked for anything other than sex from Olivia, and she loved it that way.

Realizing that she was on the verge of losing complete control, Olivia knew she had to act fast before giving into her body's natural desire.

"Go home to your wife," She snapped as she stepped away from Nick's embrace. "Show her just a fraction of the attention you gave me and try to salvage your marriage. I'm sure you have to be tired of doing this."

Nick pulled Olivia back in and started kissing and touching her as if he hadn't heard a word she had just said.

"Stop, Nick," Olivia stated with her mouth. Meanwhile the change in her body movement as she sunk deeper into his embrace told him to do otherwise.

Once she realized he wouldn't be the one to make the first move, Olivia forced herself to pull away from him.

"Stop this bullshit," he responded forcefully. "I haven't had any all fucking week, and I just want to cum damn it. I don't say anything about this weird as schedule you have. I know you are busy, and that is why I settle for whenever you pop in here. But sweety you already know what's up."

Is that all I am to him? She questioned herself as he wore his evident frustration on his brow about her change in demeanor. *I mean sure, I said that I preferred a clean break from the emotional ties, but for some reason I'm not flattered by him seeing me as some sex object that he can use whenever he sees me around.*

"I mean it, Nick," Olivia stated boldly. "I'm not interested in helping you get off, but I'm sure your wife would be willing to do that for you if you would just give her a chance."

"You know what's funny to me," Nick started. "We've been fucking for all of these years, and you have never given a shit about her. Hell, you've fucked me in her car and on the bed I share with her. Suddenly, you want to pretend like you give a damn about my marriage," Nick chuckled. "If something else is going on with you, I can understand that. But you are not going to use my marriage as the excuse when it has never been a problem before."

Nick was right. Before this moment, Olivia didn't give a fuck about his marriage. *How the hell am I supposed to tell him the real reason I don't want to do this, if I can't fully admit it to myself yet?*

Suddenly, as if Olivia was on the set of a bad episode of Love & Hip-Hop, Nick's wife, Vanessa, appeared from behind the decorative curtain that separated the office from the store.

"So, you're the bitch I've been sharing my husband with for the last five years," she said as the anger and pain oozed out of her. "This is how I finally get to meet you."

Olivia had never seen Nick's wife before. Truthfully, before this moment, all she cared about was the curve of his dick that hit her G-spot, but now staring face to face with her fellow Latina, she felt terrible.

"I've been sneaking in every day this week, waiting for a chance to finally meet the woman who has her share of blame for the failure of my marriage. I have to say I'm shocked. Certainly, I expected you to not look so bland."

Olivia was not afraid of anyone, and she never backed down from a fight, but how could she stand up for herself when she knew she was wrong here? *She's already hurting. There is no reason to throw around insults with this woman. Just let her have it, Liv.*

"After all this time, I'm finally staring into the eyes of the woman whose name I only know because my husband screams it out in those rare moments when he does decide to finally fuck me. Do you have any idea how the hell that feels?"

Olivia stood, frozen and silent. *I'm sorry won't work because before this moment I didn't give a damn. Anyway, what the hell does she really expect me to say to her right now?*

Vanessa was a small woman with a chest the size of a twelve-year-old boy and very small hips. Her frame was the complete opposite of Olivia's thick in the right places and busty figure.

Despite Vanessa's jab at Olivia's looks, Olivia knew better than to take what she had to say personal. Olivia Perez spent way too much time training for long sexual escapades and rendezvous to not have the body to show for it.

Vanessa wore a buzz cut, while Olivia's thick curly hair fell down the middle of her back. Nick loved wrapping his hands around Olivia's. He said it was easier for him to be in complete control while he grabbed her wide hips and fucked her from behind. Even though Vanessa had a beautiful face, Olivia couldn't see a single thing that he would be attracted to in his wife.

"You have no right sneaking into my business to check on what or who I'm doing. Our relationship is over," Nick said firmly as Vanessa never once moved her gaze from Olivia's eyes. "Get the hell out of here, and when I get to my house, I want you and all of your shit cleared out."

"I know what you're thinking," Vanessa said, not bothering to acknowledge what Nick had just demanded. "What could this gorgeous, successful man who is amazing in bed see in this frail, bald-headed woman before you? Well, I didn't always look this way.

Unfortunately, once chemo started robbing me of everything that my husband once loved about me, he found comfort and pleasure in a cheap replacement. It was hard enough losing my breasts and hair while fighting for my life without having to lose my husband and best friend in the process."

Olivia was disgusted in herself. How could she have participated in killing the spirit of her fellow woman when she was already battling with a disease that was killing her beauty and body? *I didn't know,* Olivia tried reasoning with herself as she wrestled with the idea of what she could say back to Vanessa.

"I'm sorry, I had--" was all she could say before Vanessa rudely interjected.

"Save your fake ass apology for the other homes I'm sure that you're wrecking. Listen, if you truly mean what you were about to say, get the hell out of here and never come back. Forget about Nick and whatever is what that you shared. Leave him alone to figure out this next chapter with the woman that he already committed to doing life with." Vanessa pleaded.

Olivia didn't bother to object. Without saying another word, she quickly walked in the direction of the door.

"Call me please," were the last words she vowed to ever hear from Nick's mouth again.

***

"I'm Carla, and I'm a grateful recovering sex addict," the large round woman who stood up confessed to the small group. "I knew that I had an addiction to sex when I was only thirteen, but it was something my friends and I would laugh about. I guess I should have known my addiction was unhealthy when I got pregnant from an orgy I had with my sister's boyfriend and my mother's husband.

They just bragged about what amazing lovers their partners were, and I just had to find out for myself," Carla confessed. After answering the question that was the topic for the evening, she sat back in her chair.

All of the other women had shared their heartbreaking stories of when they realized how severe their addiction actually was.

Then, Daniella stood up. "This is a judgment-free zone, so no one ever has to worry about what is confessed with us. We are all here to help each other through this."

With sweat soaking her palms and feet, Olivia stood up to face the women who had been comfortable enough to share their stories with her. She stood awkwardly for a moment and never once removed her eyes from the floor when she finally confessed aloud what she had already accepted as truth.

"My name is Olivia Perez, and I'm a sex addict."

2

PLAYING WITH FIRE

"You made some powerful confessions last night," Daniella said happily. "I'm super proud of you."

"Yeah. Yeah. Yeah," Olivia replied nonchalantly. "Can we just get on with your vast number of questions for the day? I have shit to do you know?"

"Sure, we can, but first, I want to try to understand your temperament change. I know this isn't going to be easy, but you were eager for help and treatment last night," Daniella stated. "Today, your body language and attitude seem very insouciant. What's going on with you today?"

Olivia wasn't ready to begin treatment so fast - even though everything from the day before proved she needed it as soon as she could get it. Laying alone in her large California King bed for the first time in years gave Olivia a full eight hours to think about how sex had come to ruin her life. She had allowed her addiction to cost her friendships, family members, and even some clients. Having the time to reflect on all of that while she laid there alone proved to be much harder than Olivia could have ever imagined.

"It's just been a really rough twenty-four hours," she replied as she slumped down further on the couch and adjusted the large sunglasses she was wearing. "I think making these confessions and coming to these realizations has just been a very exhausting process. I'm not sure if that makes sense to you or not, but that's just how I

95

feel."

"Honestly, it's going to get worse before it gets any better," Daniella responded back. "But you must remember that it will get better. Treatment is going to require you to relive some memories that I'm sure you've buried away in the back of your mind somewhere. It's not going to be an easy process. I won't lie to you about that.

There will be days where you will feel great and accomplished. Then, there are going to be days when you want to just throw in the towel. Healing the traumas that occurred in your life as a child takes a lot of energy and dedication."

I wish my mind would allow me to forget all of the traumas that have probably contributed to why I am the way that I am now, Olivia thought to herself. *Maybe that would make this whole healing process much easier for me to actually deal with.*

***

Olivia and Daniella had agreed that it would be best for her to try to get some rest, so Olivia decided to go home and do exactly that.

In an effort to avoid her clients that she was sleeping with, Olivia had to have her assistant, Lily, taking all of her calls and appointments so she could take some time to just lay low. Even though that was completely usual for her.

Olivia had built her PR firm, Perez's Public Relations, from the ground up right after she graduated. The thought of not overseeing the day-to-day operations made her stressed enough to need some dick. Even after working non-stop for the last ten years, Olivia was struggling to accept the fact that she needed this two-month vacation that Daniella had just recommended.

Devon, Walter, and Jordan were a few of the amazing partners she hired who even had to fix a few of her own messes, so her company and clients were in great, big, strong, powerful hands.

The thought of Devon reminded Olivia of his large hands. It brought back the memory of his fingers wrapped firmly around her neck when she had officially welcomed him to the office. That alone was enough to get her so hot and wet that she immediately needed a cold shower to cool down.

The freezing water did precisely what she needed it to, but she felt so alone in her large walk-in shower. Most of the time, she was accompanied by Francisco, Bryan, John, Jacob, Nick, Kevin, James,

Michael, Joseph, Daniel, Charles, or any of the dozens of men she had been sleeping with throughout the years.

She slid her hand down her large wet breasts to feel just how hard her nipples were. Next, she slid them down her well-toned body to find the part of her that had been neglected for what felt like far too long. Even though the water felt like ice on her smooth caramel skin, her center was warm and eager to be played with.

"It's important that you not engage in any kind of sexual activity," Daniella's voice rang through Olivia's head just as she slipped her two fingers inside of herself. "That means that you shouldn't even entertain sex by yourself either."

Frustrated, she pulled her fingers out, shut off the water, and grabbed her towel. She stepped on the plush rug and was surprised to hear rustling sounds coming from the other side of her bathroom door. Quietly, she tiptoed to the door and nervously swung it open.

On the other side was a burly 6'5 man standing in her master bedroom by the air vent.

"I'm sorry, ma'am," the man in the brown maintenance uniform stated sincerely. "We left a note on your door that we would be in your home today since some of your neighbors are having issues with their A/C units. We just want to be proactive in preventing a problem for you."

Olivia didn't doubt what he was saying. She was so used to getting flyers on her door that she never really paid attention to them, so it wasn't any different today.

"Oh, that's OK," Olivia stated as she took her towel off to reveal her naked body. "I hardly ever pay any attention to those things to be honest. Do whatever it is that you have to do, and please don't mind me at all."

Most women would have been terrified of the gorgeous giant that stood in front of her, but the scent of his musky cologne had drowned out Olivia's better judgment.

She grabbed the bottle of baby oil from her nightstand and laid out on the bed to rub it all over her naked body.

"I can always come back some other time, ma'am," the man responded as he did his best to avoid starting. "I'm honestly not trying to intrude." Apprehensively, he looked away and held his hands up to block the view of her.

She knew she was turning him on by the slow rise of his member in his too-tight uniform, but when he went to adjust himself, she saw it: his wedding ring.

All Olivia could think about at that moment was the hurt look in Vanessa's eyes from yesterday. Once again, Olivia could feel the embarrassment of being a homewrecker for a woman that could already be struggling with her life or marriage.

She immediately stood up, grabbed her towel, and wrapped herself up.

"I think that would be best," Olivia snapped back at the gorgeous giant. "Grab your things and leave, please."

Without disputing, he grabbed his toolbox and quickly left her to sulk in her large condo all alone.

***

"You know, my assistant has this fantastic job of making appointments. It makes it so much easier for all involved if I know what time to expect you," Daniella stated sarcastically. "As a matter of fact, that is part of the whole reason I hired her. You really should give that a chance."

"I'm ready to talk now," Olivia said as she flopped down into the leather couch, uninvited for the second time in only two days. "I'm tired of dealing with some of this shit on my own. Maybe it would be helpful to get it off my chest."

Daniella grabbed her notebook and pen and headed for her seat across from Olivia. "What is it that you're so eager to share with me today," Daniella asked.

"I'm no doctor, but I've had a lot of alone time to think things through, and I think the fact that my dad wasn't around has a lot do with my sexual addiction. Maybe it was the rejection that I felt from him that had me searching for love and affection from men who would never be able to give it to me."

Daniella put down her pen and looked up from her notepad.

"I won't argue with you there because a father's role in his daughter's life is critical. Despite that, I think that there has to be something in conjunction with that," Daniella stated. "Some of my colleagues might tell you that you simply have a biochemical abnormality and write you a prescription for an antidepressant or some other kind of psychotropic medication. That could very well solve the problem. My experience with this disease, however, stems typically from something else.

Sex addicts usually come from dysfunctional families. One study found that over 80% of sex addicts report suffering from sexual abuse as a child. For that reason, I usually like to go down those possibilities first before I suggest seeing a shrink that can write a prescription that could do more harm than good."

"Wait. So, there is a possibility a pill could make these ungodly urges go away, and you're holding out," Olivia asked as she sat up in her seat. "I thought you wanted to help me?"

Daniella chuckled a little before she responded. "Like I said, it is possible that a simple pill could fix it, but that's not always the case. Not to mention, experimenting with drugs that could alter your brain's chemical balance could do way more harm than good if you take the incorrect medication.

I had a patient once whose brain thought that sex was crucial for her survival. The part of her brain responsible for her rational thinking and better judgment would tell her that having wild illicit sex was good. It's the same part of the brain that tells her she's done an excellent job when she eats because her body was hungry. Her brain told her it was a great thing to have sex because her body needed it like it needs food and water. That imbalance made her a perfect candidate for medication. We found that after hypnosis and a complete evaluation, we were able to rule out past abuse.

While I am eager to help you, I'm not going to suggest you do something that has side effects as severe as suicidal thoughts and actions without ruling out the other stuff first," Daniella explained as she picked her pen and pad back up.

"Do your patients who have suffered sexual abuse have an easy time talking about it," Olivia asked as she began squirming in her chair.

"Unfortunately, not always. It's difficult to relive the moments where a child's innocence is lost without their consent. Why do you ask that?"

"Because I've never told anyone besides my mother about it," Olivia replied as she shifted herself on the couch. "I won't even know where to begin, honestly."

"How did your mother respond when you told her what happened?" Daniella asked.

"My mother was great at pretending things were OK. Like when my father brought home the baby he had with his mistress, she didn't even break a sweat. All she did was prepare the baby room like she wanted the bastard in our lives. I didn't expect much from her when I told her, which I'm glad because she didn't give me shit. She made up a couple of excuses and then went and tended to some other bitch's baby. It was almost like she hadn't heard a word I said," Olivia confessed.

"I'm so sorry to hear that," Daniella started. "I know that had to be rough. When you think about that time, how do you feel about what you experienced?"

"How the hell do you think that would make someone feel?" Olivia's voice rose as she sat up. "How the fuck could my mother put the needs of some illegitimate bastard before me? How could she smile and act like I didn't tell her that the old fuck she trusted to watch me decided to use me for his own sexual pleasures?"

The tears Olivia had been holding on to since she was only five years old suddenly became too much for her to carry anymore. Right there in front of Daniella, she stripped herself naked in a way she never allowed anyone to see her before. She was vulnerable and wept every single tear that she had spent most of her life holding in.

***

It hadn't been easy, but after the tenth phone call from Kevin and a few dozen text messages from Nick, Olivia thought it was best to just start over completely. She changed her number and even had her apartment complex switch her to a small apartment on the other side of the property. That way, she wouldn't be bothered with Kevin's flowers anymore.

Daniella was proud of her as well as her new group of sisters. Most importantly, Olivia was proud of herself. She had never abstained from sex for so long in her entire life, and it was getting easier each and every day.

She opened the door to where their weekly meetings were held and was surprised to see all the balloons for the celebration. There was a table full of sweets and treats, and above it was a homemade sign that read, "Congratulations, Olivia!"

"You did it," Carla, another recovering sex addict, exclaimed once Olivia was inside. "I'm so proud of you."

"We all are so proud of you," Daniella said as she stood up to give her a hug. "The first thirty days are the hardest, and yet you've managed to make it look so easy."

The smiles on the other women's faces confirmed they were just as happy for this milestone as Olivia was. She was excited at how far she had come in such a short time, and she wasn't going to allow anything to bring her down.

***

"Ms. Perez, the doctor will see you now," the rude receptionist said before she slid the window closed to go back to her never-ending gossip.

Olivia had been in the worst pain of her life. She was tired of waiting impatiently on the cold, cushion-less chairs. All while the bitch just blabbed about everything from various reality TV shows to the man who left her to be with her best friend of fifteen years.

Girl, don't you ever get tired of just flapping your lips, Olivia thought as she forced herself to walk down the seemingly endless hallway.

After spending the night celebrating her milestone of sobriety, Olivia left the party only to be injured in a car accident on the way home.

Thankfully, the only thing seriously damaged was her brand-new C-class Mercedes. But once the adrenaline wore off, she started to feel the effects of the careless driver who ran into the passenger side of her vehicle at fifty miles per hour.

When she finally made it to the exam room, she immediately sprawled out face down on the luxurious massage table.

Not even a minute later, she heard three soft taps before the door flew open.

"Good morning, Ms. Perez," she heard a young male voice say enthusiastically.

Oh great. Here I am in the worst pain of my life, and they pair me with Doogie Howser, she thought.

"Hi," Olivia huffed through the small hole her face was resting on. "I'm in a lot of pain, and I need you to fix it now."

"I'm eager to fix that for you, but I'll need you to sit up first so I can do my initial assessment. It's the only way I'll be able to gauge your progress and see what needs to be treated first," Doogie Howser responded.

"Ugh," Olivia grunted in annoyance.

He reached out his hand to help her up, but she quickly shooed it away.

"I can do it by myself, damn it," Olivia snapped back. In that moment, all she could concentrate on was the constant pain that refused to subside. She didn't mean to come off like such an asshole, but until she could get the pain off her brain, everyone would just have to deal with it.

Olivia mustered up all of her energy and sat up. She adjusted her blouse, looked up, and then it happened.

Right there in the windows to his soul, she found herself so lost in the intense blue eyes looking back at her that she forgot everything else she was just complaining about.

Damn, she thought as she tried to pry her eyes from his even though it was all in vain. *He's gorgeous.*

"Sorry to have to meet you under these circumstances," the handsome doctor said as he pulled her out of her trance and extended his hand to formally greet her. "I'm Dr. Marcus Cannon, and it's nice to meet you."

Olivia placed her hand in his large, strong hand to return the friendly greeting, but she never once removed her eyes from his deep gaze.

"It's nice to meet you too," Olivia said sweetly. "I'm usually not such a bitch, but hopefully, you can help me change that."

"I'd love to, but my track record proves I typically have the opposite effect on women," Dr. Marcus Cannon replied with a chuckle. "I'm sorry, please don't mind me. I have an odd sense of humor. I'll try to keep it professional from now on."

Truthfully, Olivia didn't mind it at all. She appreciated the opportunity to see the perfect set of white, straight teeth he had when he started laughing.

"You call that an odd sense of humor," Olivia responded. "This should be a lot of fun."

"You're beautiful and intelligent. Your husband is a lucky man," Dr. Marcus Cannon said with a sly grin.

"With all of these jokes, I'm starting to think that you're in the wrong profession, Doc," Olivia snickered. "I'm most definitely not married."

"That's too bad," his lips said even though the tone of his voice didn't match what he was saying. "Your boyfriend really should lock you down before someone comes to sweep you off your feet. Doesn't he know that Orlando is crawling with young, available doctors waiting to meet someone like you?"

"Well, Doctor, if that's true, then I have yet to meet any of them," Olivia responded.

"You never know," Dr. Marcus Cannon stated. "One could be right under your nose."

She blushed.

"Now," he said as he walked closer to her. "I'm going to get behind you and start my assessment. I realize that you're in a lot of pain, so I promise to be as gentle as I can."

3

BURNING UP

"Liv, I can't deal with you anymore," Janet managed to squeeze in after laughing so hard.

"I'm serious, girl. *Dr. Marcus Cannon,*" Olivia joked as she tried to lower her voice to match the bass in his, "is super fine. He's 6'4 and at least 240 pounds of all man. Those piercing blue eyes, that perfect smile, his chest, his ass. Oh my gosh! What is happening to me? I've never been curious enough to try white chocolate, but honey, he could get it!"

Since they were teenagers, Janet and Olivia always got together to discuss their week over a bottle of wine and a game of monopoly. Now, instead of sneaking one of Janet's dad's cheap bottles of wine, they were drinking a bottle from the winery they both invested in when they started making money from their own businesses.

"Seriously though," Janet said once she was able to finally contain her laughter. "How does Daniella feel about this? Don't you think it's a little soon into your sobriety to be so open? Do you think he'll be able to support you through this process," Janet asked with concern.

"What the fuck can she say," Olivia spat back. "I'm a grown-ass woman, and I don't need everybody in my damn business. When I think she needs to know, I will let her know. In the meantime, I have everything under control."

"I'm sure you do," Janet started. "But I think you—."

"I said I have everything under control," Olivia declared. "Now, roll the dice and finish getting this ass-whoopin. Because I'm tired of talking about anything else."

***

"You must exercise a lot," Marcus mentioned as he worked out the last few kinks from her neck. "It's only been six weeks, and you seem to be healing up very quickly. Pretty soon, you'll no longer have to come to see me anymore."

He extended his hand to help her up from the massage table. "If you follow my last few suggestions, you'll be back to your old self in no time."

Olivia was thrilled to find out that she could have eight hours of her life back every single week. Still, she hated the idea of not having an excuse to see Dr. Cannon any longer.

She had grown accustomed to his corny jokes, and more importantly, his smile. She loved how he asked about her day and took an interest in everything she seemed to say. For once, she had allowed herself the opportunity to know something about a man other than just his penis. However, because sex was always her way to lure men in, she didn't know what to do next.

"Well, I've been doing everything else you've suggested," Olivia responded. "So, I'll do whatever you say to get right back to my old self."

"Great," Dr. Marcus said as he feverishly scribbled notes in her chart. "Also, I'm going to pick you up tomorrow night at 8:00 PM sharp. I emphasize that because I hate waiting."

***

"You look fine, Liv," Janet stated as she tried to reassure her nervous friend. "Why are you doing all of this anyway? You've been on a million dates before."

"I don't know," a frustrated Olivia shouted as she practically tore off what felt like the hundredth dress she had tried on. "I just really like this guy, Janet. Maybe there is a part of me that is scared that I'm not as interesting if sex is not on the table." Olivia's confession was heavy, but it made her feel better to admit it.

"Wow," Janet responded as she sat straight up on Olivia's bed. "I have never seen you act like this with anyone in your life. I guess that is why I didn't pay attention to how serious this could be for you."

"I know. I don't think I've ever felt this way before," Olivia responded. "And now I don't know what to do with myself. For the first time ever, I'm worrying about things I never cared about before.

What if I say something stupid? Will he like what I'm wearing? How should I wear my hair? I'm having to do all of this because I can't rely on the fact that he's never had a bitch such his dick as could as I can. I can't spend the night teasing him about what's coming later." Olivia let out a huge sigh.

"It's normal," Janet responded. "You have a crush. He makes you feel things most men can't without having to touch you. You've been more intimate with a man you've never had sex with because you let him fuck your mind first. He's played around in your thoughts, danced in your dreams, and frolicked through your memories. You've experienced an orgasm more powerful than anything you've ever felt between your thighs. That's because long after his words have subsided, you'll continuously erupt from the pleasure his skills provide. You'll never be able to let him out now. Whether he ever ends up in the treasure chest between your legs, he'll always be in your head," Janet declared.

"Damn, sis. That was deep."

"Eh," Janet responded as she casually shrugged her shoulders. "I've just gone through it enough that I know what it feels like. You can either submit and join in on the tango, or you can sit up here in this empty apartment for the rest of your life."

"That sounds so simple to you, but this is all just so new to me. The only conversations I've had with men are about business or sex. I honestly don't know what topics to bring up outside of that. What if he thinks I'm boring because of that? What if my Latina flare is too much for him? I've seen the Sports Illustrated magazines that he has hidden in his desk drawer, and I don't look anything like those skinny bitches in there. I have an attitude, flava, and these huge ass hips," Olivia stated.

"Girl, you also have your own freaking PR firm, a great heart, a beautiful face, and a slim waist," Janet said hyping her best friend up. "You better go give that man that sprinkle of Adobo his ass has been missing."

They both erupted into a fit of laughter.

"Janet, what if I slip up?" Olivia asked once the laughter finally ceased.

"You won't because you can't," Janet replied firmly. "That's why I haven't been commenting on anything that you've said regarding sex. You say that you have it under control, so I'm going to believe that you would not have put in all of this work just to give up now.

Anyway, have you shared any of this with Dr. Cannon or are you still hiding this from him?"

"No, but I will," Olivia responded back knowing that her friend was going to have something to say about her honesty.

"Liv," Janet shouted as she threw a pillow at her.

"I know. I know. I'll do it tonight."

"You better," Janet demanded.

***

"You look amazing," Marcus said as he took her hand in his to gently kiss it. "Thanks for agreeing to see me this evening."

Marcus was such a gentleman, and he cleaned up nicely. His amazing body looked great in his suit.

"Thank you for inviting me. I just never took you for a sea and soul food kind of guy," Olivia responded.

"I wanted to try something new, so I figured I'd do that with you. Do you like it," Marcus asked.

I hate this fucking place, is what she wanted to say since her good friend, Tamia Santiago, had forced her to eat at Ned's one too many times.

"Truthfully, no. Seafood really isn't my thing," Olivia stated as she slid her plate away from her. "You just seemed too excited about it, so I didn't want to ruin your night."

"Ruin my night? How the hell could you have done that? I've got the prettiest girl in the world to let me take her out. I'm already winning," Marcus responded back with cute smile. "Let me fix this. Tell me whatever you want to do, and we'll do it."

***

"Take that," Olivia bellowed. "I told you before that I am a pro at this shit," she said once she finally caught her breath.

"Damn," Marcus responded in dismay. "Who the hell taught you all of that?"

"My brother," she replied in a matter-of-fact tone. "Basketball is a family sport, so you learn how to handle a ball the moment you learn to walk."

They both laughed.

"Well, that ass-whoopin' made me hungry as hell." Marcus stated. "Where do you want to eat?"

"Well, there is this bar right down the street from here. The wings are great, the beer is better, and if we hurry, we can get the last quarter of the game.”

***

“How the fuck aren’t you married already?” Marcus managed to slur after losing track of how many pitchers of beer they had shared together. “You’re really into sports, you’re beautiful, smart, and funny. There is no way I could have found a woman as perfect as you. I keep asking myself how did I manage to get this lucky.

“Oh, cut it out,” Olivia stated as she tried to hide the fact that his last comment had made her blush. “I have my flaws just like everyone else.”

“I’m sure you do, but your flaws just seem obsolete to me because I realize how much we have in common. You have no idea how hard it was to get up the courage to ask you out.”

Olivia blushed, but she didn’t immediately respond. She couldn’t believe she had been so nervous when he obviously was interested in her just the way she was.

“Damn it. I’m blabbing. I do that when I’ve had too much to drink,” Marcus confessed.

“It’s adorable. Thank you for telling me that,” Olivia took her hand and gently laid it in his.

That one-touch was enough to ignite a fire in between her thighs. As if he had managed to feel the change in her body temperature and elevated heart rate, he leaned in and spoke low and softly. “I’m going to call us a cab and close out the tab. I’ll be right back, beautiful.”

Marcus knew how to balance being in charge and being a gentleman very well. He never brought up sex, and Olivia loved it. But there was no denying the sexual tension that was growing between the two of them.

***

“Thanks again for letting me take you out tonight. I really enjoyed myself,” Marcus said as Olivia fumbled nervously in her purse for her keys. “I almost wish it didn’t have to end.”

He stepped in closer and gently laid his hand on hers. His touch offered an alarming sense of peace and passion at the same time. Marcus leaned in closer, and with the heat from his body next to hers, she knew there would be no way to deny him or those feelings if she allowed it to go any further.

Quickly, Olivia kissed Marcus on the cheek.

"I wish it didn't either," she responded. "But I have a meeting with a big client tomorrow, and I need to sober up. I'll see you tomorrow afternoon for our appointment."

Olivia reached under the decorative plant for her spare key and was in her house before Marcus had a chance to respond.

"Good night, beautiful," she heard him say before he turned to leave her and her sexual tension for the night.

***

"I just don't know how to tell him," Olivia confessed after giving Janet a play-by-play of their date.

"Olivia, I get it, but you have to. He has a right to know by now," Janet responded.

"It sounds so much easier than it is! I thought about doing is so many times last night, and I just couldn't get it out. What if I tell him and he doesn't want to see me anymore? What is he thinks that there is something wrong with me?"

"Well, that's a chance you have to take. Dr. Marcus needs to know," was all Olivia could hear before the call started breaking up.

After moving throughout her apartment for better reception, Olivia heard Janet ask, "How does Daniella feel about all of this? I know you've been saying that you are going to mention it to her, but have you actually done it?"

"I don't really know how she feels about it, but I guess she doesn't see it as big of a deal as you do," Olivia responded.

"I know what you're doing," Janet declared. "Do you forget that I've known you for as long as I have? Does she know that the chiropractor you've been seeing is an absolute boss who happens to be attractive as hell, and now you can't stop gushing over him? Does she know that he took you out last night and that you barely escaped from your newfound sobriety after getting drunk? Does she have any idea that your hot ass is now probably going through all of the items in your closet to find the perfect one to see him today? Does Daniella know all of that," Janet asked.

Shit. She really knows me better than I ever thought.

Olivia tossed the tenth outfit she had tried on to the side before responding.

"Ok, so I did not exactly give Daniella all of those details that you just mentioned. I haven't quite told her about all of that just yet."

"Then what does she know, Olivia? And don't dare bullshit me.

109

This shit is serious."

"Well…" Olivia struggled to get out.

"Spit it out, Olivia Perez. What exactly does Daniella know about this relationship that you've been in?"

"Truthfully, I haven't really seen her much since the accident," Olivia spat out.

"What," Janet exclaimed.

"Look. I've still been attending all of the meetings, but I just don't see her that much anymore. I really think I've got this under control."

"For your sake," Janet started. "I really hope so."

4

DEADLY CONFESSIONS

"Hmm," the soft moan slowly escaped Olivia's lips as Marcus' heavenly hands worked feverishly on her back. "Your hands are so good you probably could have put Humpty Dumpty back together. I seriously hate that this is our last appointment," she said, meaning every word.

"This is the last appointment that your insurance will pay for. However, this will not be the last time you see me," Marcus said as he continued to massage her back like it was actually a part of his job description.

Olivia didn't know exactly how to respond, so she just remained silent.

He finished her massage and his final assessment. Olivia climbed off the massage table and adjusted her dress before turning to grab her stuff.

"Thank you, doctor," was all she could say before her tongue was dancing with his. Without any prior warning, he pulled her in close for the kiss he had wanted from the night before. After a few moments, he let her go.

"I'm sorry, Liv. I just can't control how I feel about you anymore. You're in my thoughts, my dreams, even my daydreams. I think I'm falling in love with you," Marcus confessed.

In all of her years, Olivia had only heard that from a man when his dick was hitting the back of her throat, or he was playing with the gem she had in between her thighs. She had never had a man love her for who she was and not just what she had to offer him sexually.

Olivia wrapped her right arm around his neck to bring him in for another kiss. This time she didn't hold back, and neither did he.

Marcus gently pushed her back on the massage table and lifted her dress. He forcefully pulled her to the very edge of the table, lifted her dress, and ripped her panties off her.

"I can't wait to taste you," Marcus said before he started kissing her just above her belly button.

"Wait," she interjected as she sat up. "There is just so much I have to tell you first. For starters, I've never really been eaten out. Most of the men I've seen have been Jamaican. My last lover use to tell me all the time, 'real badman dun eat wa he can't chew'," she said as she attempted to repeat his exact words in his native language.

They both giggled at her poor attempt.

"There are just a lot of things you don't know about me," Olivia declared.

"I have the perfect idea on how we're going to solve this problem, gorgeous. I'm going to lie back on this massage table, and you're going to hike that dress up, come sit on my face, and tell me everything I need to know."

***

"Ms. Perez," Lily, Olivia's assistant, asked after she finally got a chance to relax. "I'm just as excited as you to move the office to a brand-new city, along with the raise that came with it, but why?"

"I just needed the change. Please just get back to work," Olivia lied as she tried to burry herself back in the e-mail she was forcing herself to read.

Truthfully, she was just running away from everything. Olivia needed a fresh start.

Marcus made love to Olivia that day in his office. He made love to her until his assistant had to finally close the office down for the rest of his patients.

After they left, he made love to her on almost every square inch of her condo's floors. They turned off their phones, and for two days, they were uninterested in anything other than each other.

She cooked for him. He massaged her feet. They read and played board games. When they finally turned on the T.V, it was only to get the highlights of what they'd missed from ESPN. Everything felt perfect. It was almost too perfect for Olivia.

"Yes, ma'am," Lily responded. "I just can't help but feel like I'm missing a big part of the story. I know I'm just your employee, but I do care if everything is ok with you. If you finally decide that you want to talk about it – I'm here."

It had been five months since that weekend get-away with Marcus, and she still couldn't get him off her mind. Olivia thought moving away and starting over would rid everything she was craving from him. It seemed like that fire that burned inside her for dick had turned into something she felt only for Marcus.

She did her best to avoid him for six weeks until he finally just showed up at her door one day.

"You can't keep avoiding me. Even though you won't say it, I know you feel the same way I do. There is no way I can be feeling this alone," was the first thing he said when she finally opened the door.

She pulled him inside and kissed him passionately. She had missed him, but her inability to communicate just how she felt wouldn't allow her to tell him that.

He had come over with the intentions of having his questions answered but didn't dare to ask a thing.

They made love all night until the sun came up. She knew he had to be up early for work, and instead of waking up to make his breakfast like she did the last time he spent the night, she remained like she had been since they laid down.

"No breakfast this morning," Marcus stated at last as he finally turned off his incessant alarm. "Well, I did put it on you last night, so it's no wonder you're too tired. Have a great day, love. I'll see you tonight."

He kissed her forehead, rolled out of bed, and quickly got dressed before leaving her to wallow in her pity.

The truth was Olivia had been awake for hours. She just wasn't ready to face him directly.

Avoiding him had not been easy. She missed him more than anything and hated the idea of not being near him or seeing him smile that smile she loved. She didn't know he would have been as persistent as he had been, and now that he had caught her slipping, she knew exactly what she needed to do next.

"Well, well, well, look what the cat drug in," Daniella joked as she took her seat across from the leather couch.

"I know. I've just been swamped, but I'm finally ready to answer all of your questions. I have a lot I'm ready to confess."

Olivia was 100% honest with everything about her past. "I just don't think I'm capable of loving someone," she said in between sobs. "Just look at me. I'm such a mess."

"When you're ready, you will find someone to love, and if it's real, he'll love the bad right along with the good about you."

"I've already met him," she bellowed just before her sobs got louder.

"Wait. When did this happen?"

"He's my chiropractor. Well, he was, at least. I knew from our first meeting that he would be trouble. The way those blue eyes sucked me in and that smile that kept me hypnotized. I knew I should have just gotten out of there, but I wanted to see just how much I had learned on my journey to sobriety.

I did great at first. Hell, I did damn good, but suddenly everything I had felt for other men turned into this weird thing that I only felt for him. Suddenly, I cared about what I wore, said, looked like, and what he thought of me. I don't do those things - ever! I never cared about any of that, and then I started to only for him."

Daniella giggled. "Oh goodness, girl, you had me worried. It just sounds to me like you, my friend, are in love. It's a perfectly normal emotion to feel, and it's ok to be nervous about it.

Remember, this journey to sobriety isn't only to get you to abstain from sex but so that you'll eventually go on to have healthy and loving relationships. Do you know if he feels the same as you?"

"He does. That's the problem. He confessed to me that he was falling in love with me, and ever since then, I've just kind of shut down. I tried just disappearing by not answering his calls, text, or emails, but then yesterday, he just showed up. He stayed the night. Then, this morning, I just laid in bed pretending to be asleep so I could avoid the questions I knew were going to come up eventually."

"Ok, let's start over because I feel like I'm missing something significant here," Daniella stated.

"I met him after my accident. He was an excellent chiropractor until he took me out for an amazing date. After that, it became impossible to deny this attraction anymore. He kissed me in his office, and we had sex right there. We spent an amazing weekend together after that, and then I panicked. I started avoiding him to avoid what I was really feeling and the fact that I'm nervous that I'm two weeks late." Olivia began sobbing uncontrollably again.

Daniella sat straight up in her chair and leaned in to offer as much support as she could. "I'm going to help you out through this. Just relax and take a few deep breaths. Let me help you."

Olivia heard the sincerity in her tone, but she knew just how much her life was about to change after that confession.

"I never thought of what kind of mother I'd be. I don't even know the first thing about raising a child," Olivia continued.

"Well, how certain are you that you're actually pregnant? Didn't you use any protection," Daniella asked.

"I took ten tests just before I came in here," Olivia confessed.

"There are plenty of support groups that can help you make this transition. Being a mom is a beautiful thing. Maybe my opinion is biased since I have two of my own, but your life is going to have a whole different purpose now that someone else will need you."

The two women shared a heart-to-heart on the beauties of pregnancy and motherhood, and it did help ease some of the anxiety Olivia had been feeling.

"How does he feel about being a father," Daniella asked.

"Well, that's one of my problems. He doesn't really know yet. Everything about his life is about to change, and he doesn't have a single clue about any of it."

***

"Ms. Perez, you have a surprise visitor here to see you. He says that he must speak with you," Lily's voice sang out through the phone's intercom on her desk.

The surprise visitor wasn't on Olivia's calendar of people to see. Still, she knew it would be a matter of time before he finally found her.

"Can you please come here before you allow him back," Olivia asked

Lily was there in no time – like always. It was the reason why she trusted her the way that she did.

"As you know," Olivia said as she rubbed on her tiny baby bump. "My life is about to change in a major way. I'm not going to be able to handle this company anymore, so now you'll be taking over my position, and I'll sit back as a silent partner. Do you think you can handle everything that's coming your way?"

"Yes, ma'am," the overly excited Lily exclaimed while she stood there in shock.

"Great. You'll start immediately. My attorney has all of the documents for you to sign. I trust that you know what you're doing."

"Yes, ma'am. I do. I promise I won't let you or this empire you've built down," Lily exclaimed.

"I know you won't. I know no one is going to handle this mess like you will. You've helped me out a lot through this last decade. I honestly don't know how I would have done it all without you."

"Hearing that is so humbling," Lily continued. "Thank you. If it helps, I have a child of my own. While it may appear rocky in the beginning, it's not as much of a mess as it may look."

"I appreciate it, but it's much more complicated than you know," Olivia responded.

Sensing her mood change, Lily decided to change the topic. "There is a super fine man waiting for you in the reception area. He isn't on your calendar and says he is not a client or in need of your services."

"I was expecting him," Olivia responded somberly. "You can let him in now."

Olivia sighed deeply and turned her chair to face the opposite wall. While she was ready to finally face the music, she couldn't *literally* face him yet.

"Long time no see, stranger," he said as he walked in.

She heard him take a seat and search through a few pieces of candy from the crystal bowl on her desk.

"So, I take it that you're not ready to look at me. It's cool. If I were you, I probably would have found a much better hiding place if I was really trying to avoid all of this."

He was right. She didn't do a great job of hiding. Hell, if she really wanted to start over again, she could have. She had cleaned up way too much money for her good friend Tamia Santiago, so she knew she was one call away from a brand-new life in a brand new country. While she thought about doing that every day since she left Daniella's office, she knew it wasn't right to do this to her new family.

"What bothers me is that you didn't even have the decency to just end it like the woman I thought you were," he continued.

That jab hurt Olivia to hear. During the entire five months she took to herself, she realized that after three and a half decades on this

Earth, she still was unsure of what kind of woman she actually was.

"Can we just get on with this? I have a lot of things to stress about already, and I am not ready to add to it with your petty comments," Olivia spoke up.

"I really loved you, and I wanted us to work together. Didn't I make you happy at all during the times we spent," he asked hoping to finally find some sort of closure from her.

She didn't answer.

"I don't know why I expected anything different from you even after me spending all of this time trying to find you. I really do love you even though the feeling is not mutual. Isn't it crazy that even in this situation, I'm still so concerned about you," he continued.

She heard him get up.

"Olivia Marie Perez, you are under arrest. You have the right to remain silent. Anything you say can and will be used against you in a court of law. You have the right to an attorney. If you can't afford one, one will be appointed to you."

She had heard him recite the Miranda Rights at least a hundred times before. Of course, it was much more enjoyable when she wasn't being arrested for failing to disclose she was HIV positive before having unprotected sex with someone and confessing it to her doctor. After that heart-wrenching day when her best friend delivered the news that she, in fact, had contracted the disease, she started seeing Daniella to cope with the drastic change in her life. She knew that telling her about having unprotected sex with Marcus would break their confidentiality agreement since she was risking the lives of others. Still, she had to come clean to Marcus and didn't have the guts to do it herself.

Kevin reached out for her hand, and Olivia didn't resist.

"The undercover car is in the back to help keep the heat off of you. As long as you don't act crazy, we can just walk out of here peacefully and casually. If it helps any, I didn't speak up that I know I was one of the two men that you had sex with since you found out."

He stared at her in hopes that she would cry or show some kind of emotion. Yet it was evident, after all of the years Kevin had been dealing with her, he clearly didn't know the woman he claimed to be madly in love with. To her, crying was a weak trait, and while Olivia Perez was a lot of things, she was far from a weak woman.

COMING SOON:

Continue reading for a snippet from the highly anticipated collection of short stories featuring debut author Nenshia Daniels.

When a Woman's Fed Up: a Collection of Short Stories
BY: NENSHIA DANIELS

BANG! They both took a deep breath. BANG! Brenda's ears rang as she stumbled the three feet to the bathtub and rested her tired body on the edge. Her eyes filled with tears, blood gloving both her hands; she dropped the gun.

***

The first time he saw Brenda McClain was on a Monday. Mondays were her favorite days. He watched through the window as she made her way across the parking lot, hopping over water puddles created in the spring rain. He was intrigued by her youthful nature. Barging into the café doors, Brenda shook her umbrella dry and rushed through the café to the back.

"Good morning," she smiled softly as she walked by his table. He gave a polite nod of acknowledgment and allowed the moment to breathe before he turned, watching her until the 'Employee's Only' door obstructed his view closing behind her.

"It's Money Monday!" Brenda said excitedly. Sam had just arrived moments before, and they both rushed to put on their hairnets and wash their hands.

"If you say so. I'm not as addicted to fantasies as you are, so it's just Monday for me," Sam smugly replied.

"I'll take fantasy over misery any day. You're just as bitter as an unclaimed baby-momma," Brenda laughed as she looked in the mirror, ensuring her collar was straight.

"Who's the guy sitting at table 12? His face looks familiar, but I

119

can't place it." Brenda asked.

"That's not my table. Why would I know who's sitting at it?" Sam answered.

"Because you're nosey and watch all the tables," Brenda clarified.

They emerged on the floor and scanned the dining room. The busy Monday traffic of the café was heavier than usual. They both smiled with anticipation of hefty tips in the morning rush. Being nosey, Sam looked over to table 12.

"Oh, that's that one guy that always sits in the back corner in Tasha's section. I don't know why he's sitting by the window today. I hear he's a good tipper though," Sam shrugged, informing Brenda before they parted ways to work their tables.

"Good Morning, Sir. It's a good day to have breakfast at NuBees cafe! What can I get for you?" Brenda smiled. She was being as fake as the day is long, but even her disingenuous smile was beautiful enough

to capture his attention.

"Are you this friendly to all your customers?" he asked, looking back down at his menu.

"Only to the ones who are as handsome as you," Brenda flirted.

"Or only to the ones that Tasha tells you tips well?" he said as he lifted up his head to make eye contact with her. Brenda was busted, and the only response she could think was to snap out how Tasha didn't tell her anything. Sam did. So, she elected to give a halfhearted laugh and lift her notepad and pen to indicate her readiness to take his order.

Assured in the accuracy of his assessment by her lack of response, he continued, "So waitresses and strippers scout the floors the same, huh?"

Not sure if his statement was meant to be an insult, Brenda cautiously asserted, "We have assigned tables, so there is not much to scout. But if like strippers, you prefer certain waitresses, I can get permission for Tasha to serve you." "No need. I'm sitting in your section today. You will serve me today. Two eggs, an English muffin, and a small coffee." he said.

Brenda confirmed his order. "Coming right up," she said as she walked away. A few seconds passed, and he turned again to admire the whole of her short, curvy frame, his imagination defining lines that could not be seen through her black slacks and loose-fitted work shirt. Tasha and Brenda crossed paths for the first time.

"Hey, Tasha! It's Money Monday!" Brenda greeted her.

"I know, right? And I see one of my regulars is sitting in your section today. He's weird but just be polite, and he usually tips $20 plus the change from his food," Tasha coached.

"Yeah, he said earlier waitresses and strippers work the floor the same, and I was only nice because you told me he tips well," Brenda said.

Tasha laughed. "He was right. Go get your tips!" Giving Brenda a playful tap on the titty. They both walked away with a staged haste as they noticed their manager's car drive into the parking lot.

"Would you like cream and sugar for your coffee, sir?" Brenda asked as she placed his breakfast in front of him and poured his coffee.

"Yes, please. Two of each. And I am left-handed, so place my coffee and utensils appropriately going forward," he said.

"Yes, sir," Brenda promptly replied, correcting the curious look on her face before her manager walked by. Amid the hustle and bustle of the Monday morning rush, Sam and Brenda got a momentary break at

the counter as they waited for their next orders to come up.

"Table 12 is weird. His beard is shaved too perfect, and he told me to set his table left-handed going forward," Brenda gossiped to Sam.

"Going forward? So he has a new seat now?" Sam joked. "At least you don't have to deal with that one kid who thinks farting is funny. I'm just waiting on the day he sharts instead of farts." They laughed and took their orders to their tables.

"How was your breakfast?" Brenda asked as she handed him the black leather receipt holder.

"It was fine, thank you. Bring me a cup of ice water to go, please," he said.

"Yes, sir," Brenda complied. Returning promptly, walking up from behind as he put on his jacket Brenda said, "Excuse me. Here's your water, sir."

"Thank you. You can keep the change as part of your tip. Have a good day," he said as he took the water from Brenda's outstretched hand and left the café. Brenda took the receipt holder and placed it in her pocket as she cleaned the table before cashing out all her customers. She opened the leather holder from table 12. The meal was $5.17. He had paid for the meal with a hundred-dollar bill and left a twenty-dollar tip.

"Sam! Pssssssst Sam!" Brenda whispered loudly across the serving counter.

"What?" Sam yelled back.

"Come here. And shh!" Brenda said.

"How you expect to have a private conversation in the middle of a café floor, I don't understand. But we can whisper if that makes you feel better," Sam said.

"Just shut up and listen. Do you think Tasha would do something strange for a little piece of change?"

Brenda asked softly, lowering her chin and speaking into Sam's chest.

Sam burst into laughter at the question, "I don't know Tasha to know what's strange or what can be done for solid bills over change. Where is this craziness coming from?" Sam asked.

"Weirdo at table 12 left me a twenty-dollar tip AND let me keep the change from his meal!" Brenda explained.

"So, what's the issue" Same started.

"His meal was $5.17, and he paid with a hundred-dollar bill." Brenda, wide-eyed, interrupted.

"Oh yeah. You just sold some vagina. What did you do when he handed it to you?" Sam asked.

"He didn't hand it to me. He asked me to go get him some water. I did. When I came back, I handed him the cup; he told me to keep the change and have a good day. He left the receipt book on the table," Brenda defended herself.

"Oh, he's smooth. He bought you and left before you even knew you had been bought," Sam laughed.

"He hasn't bought anything!" Brenda said as she processed his receipt with the twenty-dollar bill, keeping only the change from that as a tip. She folded and placed the hundred-dollar bill in her back pocket, rushed back out to the floor to return receipts and credit cards, and prepared for her next round of tables.

Her shift ended, and Brenda smiled as she tiredly plopped down into the front seat of her car.

Two hundred and six dollars she counted out in the rainy parking lot. It had been a great Monday for her. Suddenly, she remembered him and the hundred-dollar bill resting in her back pocket. His tip was half of what she had earned the entire day. She took the folded bill and placed it in her glove compartment. Too prideful to keep it, she kept it in her car to return it whenever she saw him again.

***

Twenty-three years old and full of youth, beauty, optimism, and ambition, Brenda worked hard at Café NuBees. There were stories of business owners and executives hiring out of NuBees for positions that could open countless doors. There were also stories of NuBees being a hiring pool for glorified assistants. Either way, Brenda was positive that she was in the right place to land a job. She dreamed of being an architect and was almost done with her schooling; she worked at the café in hopes of meeting someone who could employ her by the time she graduated.

It was another Monday, and shortly after she arrived for her shift, table 12 walked in the door. She noticed his frame and positively recognized him as he sat down at table 12. Before clocking in, she ran out to her car and grabbed the folded bill that had been sitting in her glove compartment for a week. Finally, she could get rid of this dirty money.

"It must have been good! He's sitting back at table 12!" Sam taunted Brenda as she rushed around the counter to get an order.

"Shut up!" Brenda laughed back in agitation.

"Good morning, sir. Before I take your order, I have something that belongs to you." Brenda announced as she placed the folded hundred-dollar bill on the table near his left hand. "I want to make sure it's as easy as possible for you to pick back up what you dropped last week."

He smirked, "I didn't drop this. I remember placing this in a receipt book to pay for my meal."

"Yes, sir. But your meal was only $5.17. There is a thin line between generosity and propositioning. And I do not have any vagina for sale, so like I said, I'm returning what you dropped last week. Now, what can I get for you?" Brenda asked.

He smirked as he recognized Brenda's attempt to assert some authority. At her return, he stood and grabbed the receipt holder and water from Brenda.

"Thank you for your service," he said as he watched Brenda watch him place a twenty-dollar bill into the holder to pay for his meal.

"Keep the change as part of your tip," he said as he walked off with a smug grin. Feeling as though she had established control in her exchange at table 12, Brenda cashed out the ticket and kept the change from the twenty as a tip. Returning to clean off the table, Brenda rolled her eyes and quickly scanned the parking lot to see if table 12 was, by chance, still outside. She didn't know what type of car he drove and did not see his familiar frame anywhere in the parking lot. He must have been gone. Under his plate were ten new hundred-dollar bills and the folded one she had returned to him earlier underneath a card with a phone number and 'proposition' written on it. Outraged, Brenda asked for a break and stormed to her car to call the number.

"Hello," he answered after the third ring.

"I don't know who you think you are, but you really must be stupid to try and buy sex and leave evidence. I can call the police right now and report you!" Brenda argued.

"Well, that would be stupid if I were propositioning you for sex. Would you like to calm down and hear the proposition, or are you committed to the rage of your assumption?" He calmly replied. Her silence and heavy angered breathing gave him permission to continue.

"I'd like to give you a job. I would require that you start immediately. The thousand dollars is a sign-on bonus if you choose to take the position. It is an executive assistant position and would require some travel," he offered.

"Executive of what?" Brenda inquired.

"A business," he said sharply.

"When you say immediately, what do you mean? No, wait. This is weird! I don't even know your name. Come get your money and stop being weird before I call the police on you!" she said.

"Okay. No problem. I'll see you shortly," he said and hung up the phone. About one minute later, as Brenda still sat in her car trying to process this conversation, table 12 emerged from the back of a black Suburban. He was being chauffeured, and as the driver closed the door behind him, Brenda jumped out of her car to catch his attention before he entered the café.

"Hey! Proposition guy! Over here!" she yelled.

He turned and smiled with delight that Brenda was outside the café where the environment's pressures were relieved. He walked over and greeted her with a simple head nod as she unfolded her arms to hand him the eleven hundred dollars he had left on the table.

"Here's your money, and you should stop sitting in my section when you come here," Brenda demanded.

"You have a bold mouth, don't you?" he laughed.

"And you have a bold attitude to think I'm going to be propositioned, for anything, by a complete stranger." She snapped back.

"I simply observed some traits in you that would serve my business well and offered an opportunity," he responded.

"You didn't even tell me your name or what it is that you do," Brenda said.

"I am a veterinarian, and you can call me Sir. Yes Sir, no Sir, Mr. Sir, whatever feels right for you." Sir said.

Brenda squinted her eyes and thought through the situation. *What type of veterinarian has a chauffeur?*

She was convinced, "You fit the exact profile of an introverted functioning sociopathic murder. No vet can afford a chauffeur, and nobody's momma would really name them Sir. Excuse me, *Sir.* I need to get back to work." Brenda closed and locked her car door and pushed past Sir to head back into the cafe.

As she walked past, Sir gently grabbed her hand, "You are assertive and bold. I like that. It can serve you well in business but only if you are in an environment that will teach how."

Brenda looked down at her hand in disapproval at the physical contact and politely pulled away.

"I have to get to work. Have a nice day," she said softly as she turned to walk towards the café.

"You do the same." Sir smiled as he waived for his door to be opened.

Brenda was all together excited, offended, suspicious, hopeful, and angry. Was this real life? What she wanted was left under a plate of toast crumbs with bait money. She had imagined a job opportunity coming through months of conversations leading to an invitation to apply. Under a plate, though? She rushed back into the café and washed up to prepare to serve the next table.

Lost in thought, trying to unconfuse her feelings on the morning interaction she had had with Sir, Brenda half-heartedly finished her shift and drove home.

When she pulled into the parking space of her apartment, she let her seat back and stared at the dotted details of the cloth ceiling of the car.

"I don't want to get trafficked, Lord. If this man is a pimp, please weaken his hand. It feels so strong right now," Brenda prayed as she gently rubbed the palm of her hand where Sir had held her. His touch was memorable because it was firm but gentle. When he grabbed her hand, he did it so softly but restrained her with such ease. He handled her as a doll that he might break if he touched her with his power. After an entire shift of thoughts and trusting in her pimp protection prayer, Brenda picked up her phone. It was 4:28 pm - still business hours. She redialed the number. It rang two times.

"Hello, Brenda," Sir said directly.

"Hello, Sir," Brenda replied.

"Are you calling to accept my proposition?" Sir quickly questioned before Brenda could say a word.

"Yes - as long as I can get clarification on some things. What is the formal interview process? What are my job responsibilities? What is my pay rate, and can I get direct deposit?" Brenda snapped backed.

"I will text you an address that you will report to at 9 am. Be dressed professionally, and be sure to have your I.D. and an updated resume. Your job responsibilities will include anything needed to assist me in my role as an executive. Your pay rate will be negotiated at the time of your formal interview based on your interview and resume. And establishing direct deposit is standard practice immediately upon hire.

Is there anything else you need clarification on?" Sir asked.

"No, Sir. Thank you. Have a good evening," Brenda said with a puff of authority.

"You have a nice evening as well," Sir subtly laughed back.

Sir enjoyed frustrating Brenda, and she knew it. She closed her eyes and took a deep breath before allowing herself to release a huge smile. She had a real job interview in the morning! Brenda made up her mind that she would take a cautious chance at this opportunity.

ABOUT REBEL FOXX

Rebel is a freaky mom who likes to enjoy her kinks anonymously.
To escape her everyday life as a mother and employee, she enjoys writing
things she would never have the guts to say in person.
If you're a fan of her work, you can show your support by encouraging a
friend to read one of her stories.

ABOUT KEAIDY BENNETT

Keaidy Bennett is a best-selling author and the owner of LexxiKhan Presents Publishing, a female owned publishing company located in Longwood, Florida.
When Keaidy is not with her kids, you can find her reading, writing, or finding ways to help her community. If you want to connect with her, make sure to follow her on Instagram @ AKAWORDS

To book Keaidy or send her a message, you can follow her on Instagram:
www.instagram.com/akawords

www.ingramcontent.com/pod-product-compliance
Lightning Source LLC
Chambersburg PA
CBHW071944190726
48293CB00004B/1333